THE BUFFALO HUNTERS

Buffalo Hunter Dave Larabee, with two wagons piled high with dried buffalo hides, glanced at the endless stretches of western Kansas prairies and thought his load of skins represented enough money to make any man as poor as him ignore the peaceful world through which he was passing. But at least he had company on this trip. Kelly O'Brien was a green but eager young man, and a welcome assistant.

Larabee's dreamy reverie was abruptly shattered by the sudden and swift onslaught of a pack of bushwhackers. O'Brien was killed and the precious buffalo skins stolen. Larabee set out to exact his revenge, but his plans were immediately complicated by a strange combination of events . . .

Wayne C. Lee was born to pioneering homesteaders near Lamar, Nebraska. His parents were old when he was born and it was an unwritten law since the days of the frontier that it was expected that the youngest child would care for the parents in old age. Having grown up reading novels by Zane Grey and William MacLeod Raine, Lee wanted to write Western stories himself. His best teachers were his parents. They might not be able to remember what happened last week by the time Lee had reached his majority, but they shared with him their very clear memories of the pioneer days. In fact they talked so much about that period that it sometimes seemed to Lee he had lived through it himself. Lee wrote a short story and let his mother read it. She encouraged him to submit it to a magazine and said she would pay the postage. It was accepted and appeared as *Death Waits at Paradise Pass* in *Lariat Story Magazine.* In the many Western novels that he has written since, violence has never been his primary focus, no matter what title a publisher might give one of his stories, but rather the interrelationships between the characters and within their communities. These are the dominant characteristics in all of Lee's Western fiction and create the ambiance so memorable in such diverse narratives as *The Gun Tamer* (1963), *Petticoat Wagon Train* (1972), and *Arikaree War Cry* (1992). In the truest sense Wayne C. Lee's Western fiction is an outgrowth of his impulse to create imaginary social fabrics on the frontier and his stories are intended primarily to entertain a reader at the same time as to articulate what it was about these pioneering men and women that makes them so unique and intriguing to later generations. His pacing, graceful style, natural sense of humor, and the genuine liking he feels toward the majority of his characters, combined with a commitment to the reality and power of romance between men and women as a decisive factor in making it possible for them to have a better life together than they could ever hope to have apart, are what most distinguish his contributions to the Western story. His latest novel is *Edge of Nowhere* (1996).

THE BUFFALO HUNTERS

Wayne C. Lee

GUNSMOKE

This hardback edition 2007
by BBC Audiobooks Ltd
by arrangement with
Golden West Literary Agency

ISBN 978 1 405 68147 6

British Library Cataloguing in Publication Data available.

Printed and bound in Great Britain by
Antony Rowe Ltd., Chippenham, Wiltshire

THE BUFFALO HUNTERS

CHAPTER 1

Spring had come reluctantly to the grassy plains of western Kansas, but now the tiny yellow and white flowers, only grass-top high, added color to the endless green prairies that stretched to the horizon in every direction.

Dave Larabee saw the beauty with his eyes but not with his mind. These two wagons, piled high with dried buffalo hides, represented enough money to make any man as broke as Larabee ignore the peaceful world he was passing through.

Larabee glanced at the lowering sun. They weren't going to make it to Sheridan tonight. Looking back at the driver of the second wagon, he shouted at him.

"How far do you figure it is now?"

"About ten miles," Kelly O'Brien yelled back.

Larabee swung back to search the prairie stretching out before him. Half a mile ahead, the level plain broke away into a valley. That would be the Smoky Hill River. They'd camp there tonight. Sheridan was on the north fork of the Smoky Hill, which ran into the south fork east of here, perhaps ten or twelve miles downstream.

As they worked their way down a ridge between two ravines into the river valley, Larabee yelled back at Kelly again. "We'll camp on the north side of the river."

Kelly O'Brien nodded agreement. Larabee hadn't known Kelly too long, just since this buffalo hunt began a month ago, but he liked the youngster. Kelly lived in Sheridan, the western end of the Kansas Pacific Railroad this spring of 1869. His father owned a warehouse there and bought hides and sold supplies.

The river this far west was not a formidable barrier for a good team and wagon. Both of Larabee's outfits were trailworthy and crossed the stream with no trouble.

"Wish we could have made it home," Kelly said as he jumped off his wagon and began unhitching the team.

"We'll be there by noon tomorrow," Larabee said.

"If some Indians don't stumble onto us," Kelly added, glancing nervously up and down the treeless river banks. "They're all over these prairies."

"Have you had trouble with Indians around Sheridan?" Larabee asked, unhooking the tugs on his team and throwing them over the backs of his horses.

"Plenty," Kelly said.

The redheaded youngster didn't elaborate, but Larabee could hear the fear in his voice. Kelly O'Brien was barely twenty years old, lean and under six feet tall, in some contrast to Larabee's six feet two and one hundred and eighty-five pounds. Larabee was only twenty-four, but he felt like an old man when he looked at Kelly. Perhaps that was partly because Kelly had a normal home and family. Larabee couldn't remember ever having either.

As Larabee unharnessed his horses, he surveyed

the area around the camp. There were no trees or brush that Indians could use as cover, only a couple of ravines that were within rifle range. Personal danger didn't worry Larabee much, but the thought of losing these hides did. The money he'd get from them would stake him to a start in the freighting business. Once he had his own business, he'd marry Brenda Bailey and set up a home. To Larabee, that alone was worth fighting the whole Cheyenne nation for.

Larabee put the horses out on lariats, fastening the ends of the ropes securely to the wagons. The Indians' first move in a raid was to run off the horses, and a man on foot out here on this endless prairie was as helpless as a broken-winged bird in a snake pit.

"Is Sheridan half as wild as they say it is?" Larabee asked as he started a fire with some shavings he had whittled, then added buffalo chips that Kelly had gathered close to their campsite.

"I'm afraid it is," Kelly said. "Pa was in Coyote and Monument before the tracks moved on to Sheridan. Coyote was wild enough, but Sheridan is worse. I reckon that's because we've been there for a year now and still there's no law."

"Seems like they would hire a marshal like they did in Hayes."

"Can't get anybody to tackle the job. Pa is real worked up about the things that go on there. All those idle workers lying around. They just started grading and laying track again not long ago. Then there's a camp of soldiers just outside town handling the supplies shipped in on the railroad to be freighted on to Fort Wallace. But they don't keep peace; they help stir up trouble."

"Could add up to some excitement," Larabee said.

"Besides that," Kelly went on, "there's the buffalo hunters who bring in their hides, then go on a spree, and the freighters who haul in and out of Sheridan from as far away as New Mexico. What Sheridan needs is a good marshal with a dozen deputies."

Larabee put the coffeepot over the fires. "If it's that bad, I don't see why you're so anxious to get back."

"It's home," Kelly said. "There's Pa and Ma and my two sisters, Misti and Annie. Guess I'm just a big baby. But I miss them."

"Well, you'll see them tomorrow," Larabee said easily.

He didn't like blubbery kids, and Kelly was dangerously close to acting like one right now. It was because of his homesickness that Kelly had been sent with Larabee to Sheridan with these first loads of hides.

Larabee had never been to Sheridan. He had started this hunting trip from Hayes with three other men, while the fifth member of the company had gone to Sheridan to make sure they could sell their hides there when they got them and to recruit three more men to round out their crew. Kelly had been one of the men he had brought down to the Arkansas River to meet his partners. They'd had a good hunt, and the other men had agreed to send Larabee on ahead with the first hides that were cured out while the rest hunted some more and waited for the green hides to cure enough to haul in.

With supper cooked, they let the fire die down as

they ate. "Are you going back out?" Larabee asked between bites.

Kelly shook his head. "Too scary. You never know when the Indians will hit you. Are you going back?"

"That depends," Larabee said. "If I have enough money to buy into a freighting business, I'll go to work on that. If I don't, I may go back after more hides."

Larabee felt Kelly's keen blue eyes studying him. "You're not even afraid of the Indians, are you?" Kelly asked.

"Only a fool wouldn't be," Larabee said after a moment. "I've got plenty of reason to fear and hate them. I saw them kill both my parents and my younger brother."

"When?" Kelly asked.

"In '50. Pa was taking us to the gold fields of California to get rich quick. A horse went lame, and we fell behind the train. While we were resting the horses, Pa sent me for some wood so we'd have something for our fire that night. A half-dozen braves popped up out of a ravine. They demanded a lot of trinkets, but Pa wouldn't give them any. So they killed everybody and burned the wagon. I hid there in the brush along the creek and saw it all. I haven't paid back those redskins for that, but I figure I will before I'm through."

"How did you survive?" Kelly asked in awe. "You weren't very old, were you?"

"I was five," Larabee said. "I knew we were only a mile or so behind the main column, so as soon as the Indians left, I ran that way. Got into camp just after the others had had supper."

Kelly O'Brien was quiet through the remainder of

supper, apparently finding little in Larabee's story to quiet his fears. With supper over, Larabee checked the lariats on the horses again, making sure they were secure, then turned to his bedroll under one of the wagons.

Kelly crawled into his blankets under the other wagon, but apparently he wasn't ready to sleep.

"Do you believe that story they tell that Indians never attack at night?" he said.

"I reckon," Larabee replied. "Maybe they just like to see what they're doing."

"I'm going to keep my gun right beside me, anyway," Kelly said.

"I always do," Larabee admitted.

Larabee stayed awake several minutes wondering about Kelly O'Brien. Kelly had struck Larabee from the first as being a nervous fellow, given to too many fears to make a good plainsman. But now those fears seemed unduly strong, as if not getting to Sheridan tonight as they had planned was a bad omen.

Sometime in the night, Larabee awoke with a start. He lay still, trying to decide what had startled him. Everything was quiet. His first glance went to the horses, lariated to the wagon wheels. There was no moon, only the light from the stars keeping the night from being pitch black.

The horse nearest to him was looking off to his right, his ears cocked forward, his grazing interrupted. It wasn't Indians, Larabee thought. White men's horses didn't like the smell of Indians and usually snorted and tried to get away when Indians came near.

Larabee's hands crept down to the revolver he kept close to his blankets. At that instant a yell erupted that sounded much like the war cry of the Cheyennes. Three men rose up out of the grass close to the wagons.

Larabee's brain was working at frantic speed. The thought flashed through his mind again that these weren't Indians. No Indian would make a sound while attacking as long as silence would help him.

Two of the men lunged toward the wagon where Larabee was lying, and Larabee turned to meet them. The other man had disappeared and Larabee assumed that he was running toward the wagon where Kelly O'Brien was.

Larabee snapped a shot at the men and knew he had missed. The lead man had been charging toward the pile of cooking utensils that Larabee had put under the wagon a few feet from him and covered with an extra blanket. Evidently he had mistaken those pots and pans for Larabee.

Now the other man, a little fellow, dashed forward and kicked at the gun. His boot toe caught Larabee in the wrist, and the gun flew off into the grass. The first man swerved toward him, and Larabee saw the gleam of a knife in his hand. Even if these weren't Indians, they intended to make the work look like that of Indians.

Larabee threw himself to one side to avoid the knife slashing down at him. Then he was in a rolling, tumbling fight with a man as big as he was. He couldn't tell much about him except that he wore clothes like a white man and didn't smell like an Indian. But Larabee's senses had been so thoroughly saturated with the stench of the drying buffalo hides that he wasn't sure he could detect an Indian now even if he was pressed right against him. But this was not a red man. He had a neckerchief tied around his face. No Indian would do that.

They rolled out from under the wagon, and Larabee got a glimpse of the other man moving around excitedly with either a gun or a knife in his hand, waiting for an opportunity to use it.

The third man came running up, then, and leaped into the fray, grabbing Larabee by the arm and spinning him away. Larabee couldn't tell anything about this man except that he was unusually strong and was also masked with a neckerchief.

As he was pulled back, Larabee clung to his hold on the first man. But the man jerked away, and Larabee was left with only a button in his hand. He was out in the open now, and saw the big man who had just entered the fight aim his gun at him. Before Larabee could make another move, something hit him, and the world exploded in a thousand lights.

A terrific pain in his head brought Larabee to the realization that he was still alive. There wasn't much light, but what there was hurt his eyes. Still he forced them open and looked around.

Dawn was spreading its light over the prairie and slowly everything came back to him. Through his foggy thinking, he realized that he had been out for a long time. He didn't know when the men had jumped the wagons, but it hadn't been too long after he had gone to sleep.

He propped himself up on one elbow and stared around at the empty valley. The wagons were gone, and so were the horses. The cooking utensils were still piled where he had left them under the blanket. Farther over, where the other wagon had stood, Kelly O'Brien was still in his blanket.

Larabee opened his hand where something hard was pressing into his palms. In the dim light, he saw a button, almost square. Then he remembered jerking the button off the shirt of the man who had tried to knife him. It seemed to be the only thing the raiders had left to make Larabee realize they had actually been here and that this wasn't all just a nightmare. Shifting his weight, he slipped the button into his pocket.

In spite of his splitting headache, Larabee got to his knees and crawled over the grass to Kelly. There was no movement in the blanket, and he was sure what he would find when he got there.

Kelly had been stabbed several times right through the blanket. There didn't seem to be much evidence of a struggle. Likely the first stroke of the knife had ended it.

Staggering down to the river, Larabee washed his head, not being able to get all the matted blood out of his hair. But he felt better when he finished, and he could stand up without the world reeling before him.

Walking back to the scene of last night's camp, he stared around him. He had lost his hides, wagons, teams, and guns. Kelly O'Brien was dead. In the short time he had known him, Kelly had become a good friend. There would be a bereaved family in Sheridan when they heard the news. He'd have to write to Brenda that he had failed to make the stake they were looking for and the wedding would have to be postponed.

Despair washed over Larabee. He had invested everything he had in those wagons and teams, and he'd spent a hard month skinning buffaloes. Close on the heels of his despair, however, came a burning rage. Those had been white men who had raided his camp last night. He'd find them somewhere if it took him half his lifetime. He'd get his money for those skins and he'd make them pay for what they had done!

Right now, however, he had to do something with Kelly O'Brien; then he'd walk to Sheridan and begin his search for the murderers. They would be in Sheridan. There wasn't any other place for them to go with two wagonloads of hides.

The raiders had left no tools behind, so the best Larabee could to was wrap Kelly's body securely in his blanket and carry it a short distance to a ravine that ran down to the river. There he placed it against one bank and caved the bank down over it. That would have to do until someone from town came out and did a proper job.

The sun was up and getting warm by the time he had finished. Going back to the river, he soaked his head again, then struck out across the prairie, following the tracks of the wagons. He didn't even have a canteen to carry water.

He was weak, and his head throbbed until he was sick. But the determination to find the men responsible for this wouldn't let him stop. It drove him on, step by step, across the endless prairie.

CHAPTER 2

The sun climbed higher and grew hotter, and Dave Larabee's legs turned to rubber. He still followed the wagon tracks, which were easy to see, but he was sure he had come twice as far as Kelly had estimated they were from Sheridan. Now the tracks were swinging more to the east than Larabee thought they should.

Ahead and off to his left, Larabee saw the two bald knobs of the twin buttes. According to Kelly, Sheridan was close to those buttes. The north fork of the Smoky Hill ran along the north and east sides of those buttes, and the town was just beyond the river.

Far off to his left, he heard faint sounds and, stopping to listen, identified them as coming from men working with tools and machinery. That would be the construction crew building the railroad southwest from Sheridan to Fort Wallace.

The temptation to head for those sounds pulled strongly at Larabee. But these tracks he was following were made by the wagons hauling his hides. Those men on the construction crew could give him water and take him back to Sheridan after work tonight. But he couldn't wait. The only chance he had of recovering his hides was to find the men who had stolen his wagons before they got out of Sheridan.

The sun reached its zenith, and Larabee found himself moving slower than ever. The twin buttes were to his north now, and one of the knobs was almost hidden behind the other. The tracks he was following led straight east. Then they suddenly veered to the northeast and turned into a well-worn road.

Larabee studied the road. It had been in use for some time. He decided that this was probably the road between Sheridan and Fort Wallace. Soldiers and freighters traveled this road with supplies from the railroad for the fort. The wagons had turned northeast. That meant they were going to Sheridan, just as he had expected them to.

Larabee speeded up his pace as much as his throbbing head would allow. The road was well marked although not rutted as yet. Either there hadn't been much rain since this road was put to use or no wagons had traveled it when it was wet.

He drew close to the buttes on his left as the road swung north along this east side. They were bare over the top, and the rocks appeared dark like burned cinders. Larabee wondered if they might not have once been volcanoes. If so, it had been eons ago.

He suddenly stopped, for he saw something move up on the slope of the nearest of the two buttes. He shaded his eyes to cut off the glare of the sun from his left. Although Kelly had said that Sheridan was just to the northeast of the buttes, Larabee couldn't see anything yet of the town. That movement on the butte could mean Indians.

That fear passed quickly, however, for the figure up on the rocks seemed to be moving around with no attempt at stealth. No Indian would be so bold this close to the town.

There was no place for Larabee to hide if he'd wanted to. He tried to move faster along the road that passed close to the foot of the steep slope of the butte, but the extra effort only brought on his headache worse than ever. He felt blood on his neck and knew that his wound had opened up again. It seemed to bleed easily but not profusely.

He was still some distance from the hill when the person on the steep slope spotted him and began angling down the hillside at a long trot. His head was hurting, and his eyes refused to focus clear, so he didn't discover that it was a girl, and a small one at that, until she was less than a hundred yards from him.

"What are you doing out here, mister?" the girl called before she reached him.

"Looking for a doc," Larabee said.

As the girl came closer, he saw that she wasn't more than ten years old, with red hair and freckles and the bluest eyes he'd ever seen. Curiosity fairly bubbled from her.

"What hit you?" she asked.

"A bullet," Larabee said. "How far is it to town?"

"Just around this hump and across the creek. What's your name?"

"Dave Larabee. What's yours?"

"Annie," the girl said. "I've been up on the buttes. Everybody says there's rattlesnakes there, but I couldn't find any."

"You're lucky," Larabee said. He started moving again along the road that skirted the foot of the steep slope.

"I don't think I'm lucky. I never saw a rattle-snake." She suddenly reached up and caught his arm as he staggered. "Hey, you're hurt worse than you look. You can lean on me."

"I've been walking for a long while," Larabee said. "I'm tired."

"Who shot you?"

"I don't know. They jumped our camp in the dark, killed my partner, and creased me. Stole our wagons loaded with hides."

"I figured you were a buffalo hunter," Annie said. "You smell like it."

"You're quite a ways from home, aren't you?" he asked.

"Pa would think so," Annie said. "I ain't supposed to come out here. Pa says the rattlesnakes will bite me and I'll die. But there ain't nothing that little going to kill me."

"You'd better listen to your pa," Larabee said. "If a snake bite doesn't kill you, it can make you awful sick."

"No sicker than you are now, I'll bet," Annie said. "And I figure you'll pull through."

Larabee looked at the bright-eyed girl. He doubted if she missed much that went on in the town. "Did you see anybody bring in a couple of loads of hides this morning?" he asked.

She shook her head. "Those hides smell, so I don't go around much where they're unloaded. My brother is a buffalo hunter, too."

The road led down to a ford across the creek. The north fork of the Smoky Hill River actually had more water in it than the main branch where Larabee had camped the night before. Annie led the way north from the shallow ford to a spot where the creek was narrow. Two planks had been laid from bank to bank here. Annie took Larabee's hand to help steady him as he shuffled across the planks.

The the girl headed toward town, following the road that paralleled the tracks. When they passed the water tank at the edge of town where the train engines took on water, Larabee stopped and washed his hands and face in a bucket that was sitting next to the water tank.

"That ain't going to help much," Annie said. "You'd have to burn those clothes and take a bath all over to get rid of that smell."

Larabee nodded. "I know. But I don't feel like walking down the street naked just now."

Annie giggled. "That would be a sight!"

The town was divided into two sections by the railroad tracks. There was a street between the tracks and the line of buildings and tents on either side, making the rows of business places nearly three hundred feet apart. The west end of town seemed to be mostly warehouses, their platforms built out behind so wagons could load and unload on a level with their beds.

Close to the far end of the street was a two-story building on the north side of the tracks that obviously was a hotel. A huge sign hanging on its side read, "Barlow and Sanderson Stage Lines." The train depot was directly across the tracks from the hotel. A general store was on the north side, about half way up to the hotel.

Saloons lined the roads on either side of the track, sometimes elbowing one another for room, sometimes squeezing in between other business houses. A blacksmith shop was on the south side, sitting back farther from the street than the other business places. Shacks and tents were strewn haphazardly over the prairie behind both rows of business houses. The slope to the north was honeycombed with dugouts.

"Doc's office is over on that side," Annie said, tugging at Larabee's arm.

He followed her across to the north side of the track. They passed the W. H. Chick & Co. warehouse, then came to a general store. Annie led him to the east side of the store and started up the outside steps to a second-story room.

Larabee followed her slowly, his head throbbing at each step. At the top, he saw a sign that told him this was the office of Dr. Herman Epstein.

"You can make it now," Annie said. "I'd better get home or Pa will whale me good for being gone so long."

"Thanks, Annie," Larabee said. "Maybe I'll see you later."

"You sure will. I want to help you find the men who shot you."

She bounded down the steps two at a time and disappeared in the direction they had come. Larabee turned to the door and pushed it open.

The doctor was handing a woman patient a package and instructing her how to use the medicine. The woman thanked him and turned toward the door. Her nose curled as she came close to Larabee, and she brushed past him quickly and rushed through the door.

The doctor stared at Larabee, disgust appearing in his face. "Couldn't you wash before you came in?" he demanded gruffly.

"I'll take a bath after I get my busted head fixed," Larabee said. "I was shot and robbed last night."

The doctor's face softened as concern rose in his blue eyes. He was a big man, not quite as tall as Larabee but several pounds heavier. His hair was graying, and he wore spectacles that he adjusted now as he moved up to look at the wound on Larabee's head.

"It's a clean gash," he reported after a moment. "But it's got dirt in it now. It's going to sting pretty lively when I clean it out. Who shot you?"

"If I knew, he'd be dead now," Larabee said grimly. "There were at least three of them. They killed my partner and stole our wagons and hides."

The doctor put something on the gash that made Larabee wince in spite of his determination not to show any pain. "You're lucky you're alive. If that bullet had been a fraction of an inch farther over, it would have cracked your skull and you'd be as dead as your partner."

"Who's the sheriff here?" Larabee asked.

"That's a good one," Dr. Epstein snorted, and Larabee thought he detected more anger than ridicule in his voice. "We don't even have a marshal. No law whatsoever. If you've got anything to settle, you'll have to do it yourself."

Larabee nodded. "I reckon that's what I'll do, then."

"Looked around town yet?"

"Just got here," Larabee said. "A little girl showed me where your office was. Said her name was Annie. Know her?"

"Everybody knows Annie O'Brien. Her pa owns the O'Brien Warehouse down the street toward the water tank."

Larabee   frowned.   "Any   relation   to   Kelly
O'Brien?"

"Kelly's her brother," the doctor said, swabbing
something on the gash in Larabee's head and starting
to wrap a bandage around it. "Know him?"

"I met him while I was on the hunt," Larabee said
guardedly. Larabee felt that Kelly's parents had a
right to be first to hear what had happened. "Did you
notice a couple of loads of hides come into town this
morning?"

"Loads of hides are coming in all the time," the
doctor said carelessly. "I sure ain't making any count
of them."

"Have you seen any strangers in town?"

"Haven't seen anything else," the doctor said.
"Two or three thousand people in town, and ninety
percent of them are strangers to me."

Dr. Epstein finished his work, and Larabee got out
of his chair. "I'm flat broke now, Doc. But I'll pay
you as soon as I get my hides back."

The doctor shrugged. "I do a lot of work for
nothing."

Larabee went out on the landing above the steps,
frowning. The doctor didn't expect him to recover
his hides or the money for them. Larabee's jaw set as
he started down the steps. He intended to get that
money if the thieves were still in town, and he had a
score to settle with them for killing his partner, too.

He thought of Kelly O'Brien and his family. That
family would include Annie. Breaking the news to
them was going to take a kind of courage he didn't
think he had right now. He decided to look over the
town first while he built up his courage. His hand

fished into his pocket and came up with the almost square button he'd found clamped in his hand when he came to. That had come from a fancy shirt. It wasn't much to go on, but if he found a fancy shirt with a button like this missing, the man wearing it was going to have to do some fast explaining or he would wind up dead.

Larabee frowned. How was he going to kill a man? He didn't have a gun; not even his skinning knife. The thieves had done a thorough job.

He moved down the street from the general store above which Doctor Epstein had his office. There were saloons everywhere. He stopped in at a couple, the Golden Eagle and the Cross-Tie. He didn't recognize a single face among the men there, and both saloons had plenty of business. His own bandaged head didn't even cause a second look. Apparently broken heads were nothing out of the ordinary in Sheridan.

He only glanced into the lobby of the Perry Hotel, then crossed the track and started back down the street. Directly across from the hotel was the depot and next to it was another saloon. A woman, face painted until he couldn't guess her age, smiled invitingly at Larabee from over the swinging doors of the saloon, but he ignored her. Most of the saloons along the street had women like her, but he had too much on his mind to waste time on her kind.

He passed several other saloons and a few business houses, then the railroad section house. Otero & Sellar's warehouse wasn't far beyond this, and he stopped there to inquire about the hides.

"We bought six loads of hides this morning," the man in the warehouse said. "But they all belonged to one outfit. We didn't get two loads by themselves. You might try Chick across the tracks or O'Brien down toward the water tank.

Larabee thanked the man and went out. He crossed the tracks to the warehouse he had seen earlier, W. H. Chick & Co. They hadn't bought any hides since yesterday.

Reluctantly, Larabee turned toward O'Brien's warehouse close to the west end of town. He had to tell the O'Briens about Kelly, anyway. He couldn't decently put it off any longer.

He was glad he didn't see Annie when he climbed the steps to the level of the platform. He went inside the warehouse, which was on pilings, fully four feet above the ground. A middle-aged man of medium height and weight was moving some boxes. Larabee knew at a glance that this had to be Annie's father. There was the same red hair and sparkling blue eyes.

"Did you buy a couple of wagonloads of buffalo hides this morning?" he asked, stalling the inevitable moment when he'd have to tell about Kelly.

"Yeah, I did," the man said. "Only hides I've bought today. They came in early. The hunters must have camped just outside town."

"Down on the Smoky Hill," Larabee said.

"I don't recall that you were one of the men who sold me the hides."

"I wasn't," Larabee said. "But those hides belonged to me. Three men jumped me and my partner last night on the Smoky Hill. They killed my partner and creased me, then took everything we had."

The warehouseman nodded sympathetically but said nothing. Larabee took a deep breath and plunged ahead. "My partner was Kelly O'Brien."

Shock slapped the man hard, and he stared at Larabee, not moving. "You saying my boy is dead?" he said finally.

"If you're Mr. O'Brien, I am," Larabee said.

"I'm Tully O'Brien," the man said dully. He suddenly held up his hand. "Before you tell me how it happened, I want to get my family. They should all hear it."

Larabee fidgeted nervously while Tully O'Brien went out the back of his warehouse toward a small frame house standing only a short distance away. Larabee would much rather have told Tully O'Brien and let him relay the details to his family. But Tully had given him no choice.

Tully was back in record time with his family. Larabee recognized Annie, running ahead of the others, tears streaming down her face. An older woman that Larabee took to be Tully's wife was close behind. She was rather short but slim and, in contrast to her husband and younger daughter, had blonde hair. The other member of the family looked to be about eighteen and had the same blue eyes of her sister and father, although they were brimming with tears now. She had her mother's blonde hair tinted with red. Kelly's description of his sister, Misti, as an Irish beauty had not been exaggerated a bit, Larabee thought.

"Why didn't you tell me?" Annie sobbed, running up to Larabee.

"I didn't know you were his sister," Larabee explained uncomfortably. "You didn't tell me your name was O'Brien."

"Now let's hear everything you know about it," Tully said. "Where is he now?"

Larabee began with his and Kelly's trip to Sheridan, ending with the raid the night before and a description of the place where he had buried Kelly. The women's sobs were muffled while he talked, but the depth of their grief was written in their faces. This lost brother and son had been dear to his family.

"I will send the undertaker to bring him in for a Christian burial," Tully said when Larabee was silent. "Don't feel so bad, lad. It wasn't your fault."

"I've got to find the men who did it," Larabee said determinedly.

"Kelly promised to buy me a new dress when he got back," Annie sobbed.

"When I get the money from the hides, I'll buy you that dress," Larabee said. "It will really be from Kelly."

Misti wiped her eyes and looked closely at Larabee for the first time. "How bad are you hurt?"

"It's just a scratch," Larabee said. "Kind of a deep one, but the only damage is a bad headache." He looked at Tully. "Can you describe the three men with those wagons?"

"There were only two men," Tully said. "I don't pay much attention to the hunters who bring in hides. But I seem to recall that one of these fellows was heavier than average."

Larabee thought of the number of men in Sheridan and what the doctor had said about ninety percent of them being strangers. Finding three men here who had stolen two loads of hides would be like trying to pinpoint three black beans in a bag full of black beans.

CHAPTER 3

Larabee waited until Mrs. O'Brien and her daughters had gone back to the house, then he turned to Tully. He was hoping that Tully could help him in the gigantic task ahead. He knew the town; Larabee didn't.

"Any idea where I should start looking?" he asked.

"Maybe," Tully said grimly. "We'll find them, all right. Whoever killed my boy will regret the day. Would you recognize your horses?"

Larabee nodded quickly. "I sure would. The thieves are bound to get rid of them as soon as possible, too."

"That's right," Tully said. "There are men here every day trying to buy teams and wagons to go out on a hunt. If they didn't make a direct sale to some men like that, they'll likely sell to a livery barn."

"Many barns in town?"

"Three or four. The biggest one is right across the tracks from the water tank. The corral runs up the gully behind the barn. You might check there. They sold the hides to me, and that's the closest barn from here."

"So you think they might still be in town?"

"Sure to be," Tully said. "Thieves like that might even be making a business of stealing loads of hides.

They could scout each day for incoming wagons that will camp close by, then kill the drivers that night and steal the hides."

"Much of that going on?"

"Hard to say. There are more killers and criminals in this town than there are decent people."

"Want to come with me to check the stable?" Larabee asked.

Tully shook his head. "I can't. I've got to move these boxes over on the platform ready to load. Some Mexican freighters are heading for Santa Fe tomorrow. The only help I have is my clerk, Frank Woods, and he isn't much good at loading freight."

Larabee left the warehouse and went on down the street to the railroad water tank. There he crossed the tracks to the big livery barn that sat in the mouth of a gully running down the northeast toward the river.

The owner of the barn came to the front when Larabee stepped inside. He was tall and lean and baldheaded.

"Looking to buy a horse, mister?" he said, glancing around to make sure Larabee didn't already have a horse. His voice was blurred with a nasal twang.

"Just checking to see if you had bought any horses today."

"I buy and sell horses almost every day," the man said. "What are you looking for?"

"A team of bays and a team of browns with wagons. I figured you might have bought them this morning."

The man rubbed his chin. "Funny thing. I did buy a couple of teams and wagons this morning. Just about fit the description you give. You wanting to buy them particular teams?"

Larabee shook his head. "I already own them. They were stolen from me."

"You don't own them now, mister," the man said. "I paid good money for them. If you want them, you'll have to buy them."

"I'm not buying anything," Larabee said in irritation. "Can you describe the three men who sold them to you."

"Weren't but two," the man said. "Can't recall just what they looked like. See too many people every day. Seems I do recollect one man was real heavy. He was a buffalo hunter. I could smell him, just like I can smell you now."

"Was he tall?"

The man shook his head. "As I recollect, he was a mite shorter than average, but he weighed plenty. Looked stronger than a bull."

"How about the other fellow?"

"He was more of a dude. Sure looked out of place with that hunter."

"Would you recognize them if you saw them again?"

"Might; might not," the man said.

"Have you sold those teams and wagons yet?"

"Nope. You can buy them if you've got the money."

"I don't want to buy them. I just want to make sure they're the ones that were stolen from me."

"Too bad if you lost them, but they belong to me now."

Larabee pushed past the stable owner and went to

the corral behind the barn. The owner followed along as if afraid Larabee might steal the horses.

It took Larabee only a minute to spot the horses. All four were there. The three thieves were probably still in town, too. But with no better description than he had of them, it was going to be next to impossible to pick them out of this town filled with hunters, gamblers, freighters, soldiers, and idle construction workers.

He left the barn and went up the street toward the saloons again. He had one small clue to help him now. One of the men was a hunter, a short, heavyset man. There might be a hundred men in town who would fit that description, but it did narrow the field a little.

He went into the Golden Eagle Saloon again, brushing past the woman who tried to latch onto his arm and pull him toward the bar. It took him only a couple of minutes to see that there weren't any hunters there.

He checked quickly through some of the smaller saloons. Most of the hunters he saw were lean and lank, not fitting the description of the man he was looking for. Then he came to the Cross-Tie, the biggest saloon in town. It had a little more class than most of the others except the Golden Eagle, but it was even noisier. A man with sandy hair that bushed out over his head was beating on a tinny piano, and a girl, wearing more feathery frills and lace than dress, was singing in a harsh voice that cut through the cacophony of a hundred voices.

He saw several buffalo hunters, but only a couple came even close to the description the livery man had given him. Larabee moved around close to these men, making sure they saw him and watching for their reactions. Either they had not been involved in the raid the night before, or else it had been so dark they hadn't seen the faces of their victims. Neither man showed a glimmer of recognition.

Looking at the Perry Hotel just a few steps away, it struck him that men who had just sold two loads of hides might decide they should live in style. Maybe they had taken rooms in the hotel.

Stepping over to the hotel, he went inside and moved up to the desk clerk. Before he could ask any questions, however, he caught sight of someone coming down the stairs from the second-floor rooms. His mouth dropped open, and he stared in amazement.

The boarder was a girl with black hair and brown eyes, and her fashionable dress set her apart from most of the women Larabee had seen in Sheridan. She was tall and moved with a poise foreign to this frontier. When she saw Larabee, she stopped short.

"Brenda!" Larabee moved quickly to the foot of the stairs. "I thought you were in Kansas City."

Brenda Bailey came on down the steps, surprise giving way to swift action. She came into Larabee's arms but only for a moment. She drew back quickly, shock in her face.

"Where have you been, Dave? Don't you ever take a bath?"

Color flooded into his face as he remembered his clothes that were so permeated with buffalo smell. "I didn't come courting," he said lamely. "I just got in from the hunt. Last night I was robbed, and I was looking for the men who did it."

She nodded, her initial revulsion passing. "Let's go outside where there is more air. Tell me what happened."

They moved through the front door. The hotel had only a small porch, not like the huge verandahs that Larabee was used to associating with hotels. Sheridan had existed for a year now and would be here for a few months more, it appeared, until the track could be laid another fifty miles to the west. They had run out of money for construction when they reached this spot, so Sheridan had survived while more money was being raised.

Standing on the small porch, Larabee told Brenda what had happened, how he had hoped to have enough money to make a payment, at least, on a freighting outfit. Then he had planned to come to Kansas City, a successful man, and they would be married.

"Since you're still broke, I suppose our wedding will have to be postponed again," Brenda said a little peevishly.

"I can't ask you to live on nothing, which is what I've got," Larabee said. "I'm hoping I can find the men who robbed me and get my money, but that's not going to be easy in a town like this. Why did you come here?"

"I knew that you planned to bring your hides here. I thought I'd surprise you, but I guess it turned out the other way around."

"This town is no place for you, Brenda," Larabee said, looking down the street at the rough men moving in and out of the row of saloons. "You'd be safer back in Kansas City waiting for me to make a stake. Have you seen Tom Gleye lately?"

Brenda nodded. "Just before I left. There is no change. He is a total invalid except for his mind."

"Is Steve still with his pa?"

"Steve is right here in Sheridan," Brenda said. "I guess he thought he could pick up a fortune in a hurry here."

"He'll get into real trouble here," Larabee predicted, looking down the street again, wondering which saloon Steve was in.

He didn't owe Steve anything, Larabee told himself. It was Steve's father, Tom, who had raised Larabee after Larabee's parents had been killed. Tom Gleye's wife was dead now, and Tom himself was a bed-ridden invalid.

"Is Slip Neff pestering Tom for the gambling debt that Steve owes him?" Larabee asked. "If he is, I'll find that gambler and kill him."

"Neff is right here in Sheridan, too," Brenda said. "With all the money the buffalo hunters and freighters are handling here, this is a good place for a gambler."

"Especially one like Neff," Larabee said bitterly. "He'd cheat his own mother to get an extra dollar. I'm going to try to get my money back for those hides, Brenda. If I don't, our wedding will just have to wait."

"I understand," Brenda said, but Larabee detected a note of frustration in her voice.

He turned off the porch and started down the street again. As he made the rounds of the saloons now, he had his eye open for Steve Gleye and Slip Neff. They probably wouldn't be any help in locating the men he was after, but at least they could tell him if they had seen any fat buffalo hunters.

He found Neff at a gambling table in the Golden Eagle Saloon. Just as Larabee spotted him, Neff slid back his chair and went to the bar for a bottle. Larabee cut him off there. Surprise flashed over Neff's face when he saw Larabee.

"I didn't expect you to leave the comfort of Kansas City," Larabee said.

Neff stared at him for a moment. "I go where the money is," he said finally. "There seems to be plenty of it here."

"You're getting your share of it, too, I imagine," Larabee said. "One way or another."

"I don't have to cheat, if that's what you're hinting at," Neff said testily.

"Have you seen a short fat hunter here in the Golden Eagle?"

"No hunter comes in here unless he's cleaned up," Neff said significantly, looking at Larabee's dirty clothes. "If he didn't have money to throw away, he wouldn't come to my table, anyway. So I wouldn't see him."

"He probably had money," Larabee said. "He stole my loads of hides."

"Hard-luck stories don't interest me," Neff said with a shrug.

"If your luck turns sour, maybe you'll change your tune," Larabee said hotly.

"If I get down on my luck, I'll just push Steve for that debt he owes me. He's here in Sheridan, you know. If Steve doesn't come through, I'll go to his old man. He's got some property. I can collect on that."

Larabee stifled an impulse to throttle the gambler. He was a little man, weighting less than a hundred and fifty pounds. His pale blue eyes looked almost colorless from a few feet away, and Larabee had never trusted a man with eyes like that.

"You bother Tom in the shape he's in, and I'll kill you, Neff," he said sharply. "That's a promise!"

Larabee spun on his heel and went outside. If ever anybody needed killing, it was Slip Neff. But it wasn't his place to do it.

Larabee suddenly remembered that he had gone into the hotel a while ago to see if anyone had checked in recently. When he saw Brenda, he had forgotten what he was in the hotel for. He'd go back now and check. At the hotel he found that no one had checked in since the train arrived from Kansas City. Larabee turned away in frustration, heading down the street again.

As he passed the Cross-Tie Saloon close to the hotel, Steve Gleye came out almost directly into Larabee's path. Surprise flitted across Steve's face, but it passed quickly.

"Brenda said you were here," Steve said. "She also said something about a cock-and-bull story you told of losing a couple of loads of buffalo hides. You don't expect anybody to believe that you actually got that close to making some money, do you?"

Anger surged up in Larabee as it always seemed to when he was around Steve Gleye. "I don't care what you believe," he snapped. "I'm looking for the man who robbed me right now. One was a fat buffalo hunter. Have you seen him?"

"I don't pay any attention to the hunters except to stay as far away from them as possible. They all stink just like you do."

"If you don't like the smell of this place, I'd suggest you take the next train out of here."

Steve went on toward the warehouse down at the foot of the street. At the warehouse, he found that Tully had been asking questions and getting no more answers than Larabee had.

The work train came chugging in from the southwest where the construction crew was building grade and laying track. Not all workers were busy yet after the long layoff, but enough were working that the track was moving slowly to the southwest toward Fort Wallace.

One of the workers, an average-sized man with dirty grimy hands to match the dirt on his clothes, came to the warehouse. He didn't come inside but flopped down on the steps and seemed to doze off. Larabee look at him questioningly.

"That's Zeke Quincey," Tully explained. "He comes in every night with the work train instead of staying out at the construction camp. When the train stops by the water tank, Quincey gets off and comes here instead of heading for the saloons as most workers do. I'd say he is better off. By the way, I'd like to have you go with me to a meeting tonight."

"What kind of a meeting?" Larabee asked cautiously.

Tully shrugged. "A few of us are going to talk over some things. We don't have any law here, you know."

"Vigilantes?" Larabee said softly.

Tully looked around the warehouse quickly. "The rope is the only law some men respect, you know."

Larabee guessed that Tully wanted him to repeat the details of Kelly's death for the benefit of the vigilantes. He couldn't very well refuse.

He made a tour of the town with a double eagle that Tully loaned him against the wages he would earn working either at Tully's warehouse or at some other job in town. He got a haircut and a bath at the barber shop, a new outfit of clothes at one store, and a .44 to fill his holster at another. His head was still very sore, and the haircut had not been a pleasant experience, but he felt like a new man when he went back to the warehouse.

Larabee went with Tully to the meeting that was held in the back room of the barber shop. The barber, the doctor who had dressed Larabee's wound, and Frank Woods, the clerk he had seen in Tully's warehouse, were waiting for them.

Larabee soon guessed that these four men were part of the vigilante squad that ruled Sheridan with a short rope, although Woods objected every time anything was said that would indicate that they were vigilantes. Larabee was invited to join them in their search for Kelly's killer, but he didn't want to be bound by any rules the vigilantes might have when he found the men he was seeking.

He was showing the men the square pearl button he had jerked off his assailant's shirt during the fight out on the Smoky Hill River when a soldier burst into the room. Horton, the barber, and Tully reached for their guns, but the soldier was obviously drunk and apparently not even armed.

The soldier, a corporal in the cavalry, soon proved to Larabee's satisfaction that he wasn't as drunk as he appeared to be. Larabee guessed that he suspected this was a meeting of the vigilantes, but when he found only five men present, his suspicions faded.

"Just who are you?" Horton demanded, glaring at the soldier.

"Corporal Ivan Koonce. I'm on a detail to find a new freighter. One of our Mexicans quit."

"Must have been looking for him in the saloons," Woods said, sniffing the air disgustedly.

"Where else?" Koonce said. "I'm looking for a freighter, not a preacher."

"You won't find any freighters here," Tully said, and Koonce turned toward the door.

"Does this freighter have to have his own team and wagon?" Larabee asked.

"We just need a driver," Koonce said. "You looking for a job?"

Larabee nodded. "I can handle a team, all right."

"Let's go see the lieutenant," Koonce said.

Larabee followed Koonce out to the street where he had his horse tied in front of Tully's warehouse. Larabee walked beside the soldier's horse as they turned north just short of the water tank and went up the ravine. The army camp was up on the flat just above the ravine across from Cemetery Hill.

It took only a five-minute conference with the lieutenant for Larabee to land the job of driving one of the army's heavy wagons to Fort Wallace whenever supplies came in on the train.

Larabee walked back to town alone. He didn't return to the barber shop but checked the saloons again, although it struck him that the kind of man who would wear a shirt with square pearl buttons wasn't likely to be seen in public in a shirt with one button missing.

As he turned in at the Cross-Tie Saloon, he almost bumped into Steve Gleye coming out. Steve stared at Larabee and started to say something, but Larabee moved on. There was no point in asking Steve again if he'd seen the short, fat hunter. Larabee was sure it would be a longer day than he'd ever known when Steve helped him in any way.

CHAPTER 4

Steve Gleye paused at the swinging doors of the Cross-Tie Saloon and stared back at Dave Larabee. Larabee was looking over the crowded saloon, apparently hoping to see the short, heavy buffalo hunter that the livery-barn man had said sold him the teams and wagons. Steve was glad that the livery owner hadn't been able to describe the man any better than that.

Pushing on through the doors, he looked up and down the almost-deserted street. The milling throng of a few hours ago had disappeared. Those who were still up were in the saloons drinking and gambling. Inside the saloons up and down the street, a man might never guess that it was late. The crowds there were almost as big as they had been earlier in the evening.

Angling across the street toward the Bull Head Saloon close to the railroad section house, Steve pushed through the doors. This was the spot where Pete Cottier usually spent most of his time. Steve saw him almost as soon as he got inside.

This was not one of the better saloons in town, but it was just the kind Pete liked. The place had poor lights, and Steve wrinkled his nose at the foul odor that assailed him. Cottier was leaning against the bar with a woman beside him, both drinking. The woman's hair was bushing out from her combs as if she had just come in out of a bad windstorm, and her gaudy paint and powder were smeared crookedly on her lips and cheeks. Steve needed only a glance to see that she was drunker than Cottier was.

Pete Cottier wasn't a tall man. He was five inches shorter than Steve, but he was heavy. Hog-fat, Steve's father would have called him. He weighed well over two hundred pounds and every pound showed. His dirty gray hat was pushed back off his black hair, and his murky brown eyes were clouded with the effects of the whiskey.

Steve moved through the crowd as though picking his way across a pigpen. Reaching the bar, he touched Cottier's arm.

"Pete, we've got some things to talk over."

Cottier waved an unsteady hand at Steve. "Go away, sonny. I've got a man's business to tend to."

Standing close to Cottier, Steve found the added odor of the buffalo hunter almost more than his stomach could take. "You're going to be stretching a rope if we don't do something," he said.

Cottier turned then and stared at Steve. "Nobody's stretching my neck."

"You'd better come with me," Steve said, scowling. "We've got things to discuss."

"We can talk right here."

"I'm not staying in this slop hole. Come on."

"Watch your tongue, mister," the woman beside Cottier said drunkenly. "This is where I live."

Steve looked at her, his face twisted with disgust. "You look like you belong here."

The woman started around Cottier toward Steve,

but Cottier caught her arm and shoved her back against the bar where she clawed at the wood to keep from falling.

"Let him alone, Bessie," Cottier said. "He'll pull your hair out, and I don't want a baldheaded woman. Come on, Steve. Let's get this matter settled. I've got some important business to get back to."

Steve led the way outside into the fresh air, Cottier stumbling after him. Once in the night air, Cottier's head seemed to clear as he stopped and breathed deeply.

"Now what is this about a hanging?" he demanded.

"Nothing yet," Steve said. "But we've got to do something or those vigilantes are going to get on to us."

"Ain't no way they can trace anything to us," Cottier said, shaking his head.

"That livery-barn man we sold the teams and wagons to described you pretty well to Larabee." Steve glared at Cottier. "I thought you killed Larabee out there at the river."

Cottier nodded, concern showing in his face for the first time. "I thought so, too. After I jerked him away from you, I shot him. He went down like a poled ox. I don't know how he can be alive and here in town now. He must have nine lives."

"He's sure got one, anyway," Steve said. "Come on. Let's find Slip."

Steve led the way toward the Golden Eagle Saloon. He and Cottier and Slip Neff had agreed to separate and not be seen together here in Sheridan just as a precaution. The Golden Eagle offered the best gambling facilities, so Slip Neff had chosen it. Steve and

Cottier had each picked the saloon he liked best, and all had agreed they wouldn't go to the other saloons unless it was necessary to see one of the partners. Steve figured it was necessary right now.

Slip Neff was seated at a table dealing cards to two companions. Steve supposed they were getting fleeced and couldn't see how they were being cheated. Steve couldn't prove himself that Slip Neff cheated, but no man could have the phenomenal luck that Neff had without cheating.

There were two extra chairs at the table, and Steve and Cottier dropped into them. The two companions of Neff's picked up their cards, but they frowned as the strong odor of Cottier struck them. Neff scowled at Cottier, too, but he said nothing.

Steve glanced around. They couldn't stay here long. Already the big man who did the bouncing here had his eye on Pete Cottier. The Golden Eagle didn't cater to the buffalo hunters, preferring to take the money of the wealthier element and the Eastern visitors who came in on the train. The Cross-Tie where Steve did his drinking welcomed anybody who came through its doors, but the caliber of its patrons was a big step above that of the Bull Head Saloon where Cottier hung out.

At the end of the hand the two men gambling with Neff pushed back their chairs and, with a scowl at Cottier, headed for the bar. Neff glowered at the two men still at his table.

"Well, you managed to break up that game," he snapped in a low voice. "What are you doing here?"

"We have to talk to you, Slip," Steve said. "Any place where we can be alone?"

"Just keep this stinking buffalo hunter close and we'll soon be all alone," Neff said. "What's wrong?"

"Steve says the vigilantes are on our tail," Cottier said in a voice too loud to suit Steve or Neff.

"Impossible," Neff said softly, but he got up as Steve jerked his head toward the door.

Steve went outside first, but he heard Cottier right behind him. It was over a minute before Neff came out. He apparently didn't want to appear to be following the buffalo hunter outside. As the three men met in front of the saloon, Steve couldn't help thinking that this was a strange alliance, Cottier being a complete misfit in the trio. Yet he had his place in their scheme of things.

"We can't stand here in the street and talk," Neff said. "If the vigilantes have any suspicions, seeing us together would confirm them. I'll go up to my room in the hotel. You two come up later."

After Neff had gone up the street past the Cross-Tie Saloon into the hotel, Steve motioned for Cottier to start. "You go first. I'll be along."

Steve was assured that nothing would happen till he got there because he was the one calling this meeting. Neff apparently hadn't had his suspicions roused, and Cottier would never suspect anything until the rope was dropped around his neck.

Neff and Cottier were waiting expectantly when Steve knocked on Neff's door and went inside.

"Now what is this about the vigilantes?" Neff demanded before Steve found a place to sit down.

"Dave Larabee is still alive," Steve said dramatically.

"I know that," Neff said. "I ran into him in the saloon. He's got a bandage around his head, so Pete must have just creased him. But he couldn't have recognized any of us last night. It was too dark. Besides, we all took the precaution of wearing masks."

"The livery man we sold the teams and wagons to described Cottier," Steve said. "So Larabee is looking for a short, fat buffalo hunter."

"He can't prove nothing if he finds me," Cottier said.

"If he's real suspicious, he might figure a way to make you talk," Neff said, jumping ahead of Steve in his calculations.

"He can't make me talk," Cottier said. "I'll break him in two."

"You should have done that down on the river," Neff said. "If they stretch your neck with your toes barely touching the ground, you might change your mind about talking. The only thing we can do is get rid of Larabee." He glared at Cottier. "If you hadn't bungled it down on the river, we wouldn't have any trouble now."

"Don't blame me!" Cottier snapped. "I got the man I was sent after. It was Steve here that messed it up. I had to bail him out."

Anger surged up in Steve. "Slip's the one who snarled it up. He picked which man each of us was to tackle. I was supposed to get the O'Brien kid. I never could handle Dave Larabee, even when we were boys. But it was Larabee I got last night."

"All right; all right," Neff said angrily. "We're not going to get anywhere sitting here blaming each other for what went wrong. The fact is that Larabee survived, and not one of us is safe as long as he is alive. What are we going to do about it?"

"Kill him," Cottier said. "What else?"

"You don't go around just killing people here in Sheridan," Neff said. "From what I hear, the vigilantes are pretty tough when anybody gets killed right in town. They don't pay much attention to what happens out on the prairie."

"They're paying attention to this killing, I hear," Steve said. "Maybe it's because the boy was the son of one of the warehouse owners. O'Brien might even be one of the vigilantes."

"If Larabee gets to poking around too much," Neff said, "it might be safer to get rid of him even at the risk of trouble with the vigilantes. A fair fight might not be questioned."

Neff looked at Cottier, and Steve knew what he was thinking. If Cottier killed Larabee, it would be Cottier who would get his neck stretched by the vigilantes. But if they could stop Larabee's snooping around, nothing was liable to come up to connect Neff or Steve with the robbery out on the Smoky Hill. And since Cottier had been described so well by the livery man, Neff and Steve would be safer with him out of the way, anyway.

"You're the logical one to handle Larabee," Steve said to Cottier.

"Sure," Cottier said. "I do all your killing for you. But I ain't doing it for nothing. You're going to pay me for it."

"Look," Neff said, "you owe me plenty in gambling debts. Your share of the hides won't pay off that debt. But I'll cancel it completely if you get rid of Larabee."

Cottier shook his head. "You told me my share of the hides would pay the debt. That's why I went with you. You're going to pay me a lot more if I take care of Larabee now." He looked at Steve. "I know you figure to make a fortune when Larabee is out of the way. So you can kick in about five hundred."

Steve scowled. He wished Cottier didn't know so much. Neff, of course, knew the whole story; it was the only way Steve could get him to help eliminate Dave Larabee. Neff's threat to take Steve's debt to Tom Gleye had forced Steve to make a deal with the gambler. If Tom Gleye knew that Steve had run up such a huge gambling debt, he'd cut him right out of his will. And all of Steve's plans for a life of ease depended on being named the sole recipient of his father's inheritance.

Steve was sure that no one except Tom Gleye and the men in this room knew that Dave Larabee's parents had left a thriving shoe factory in Toledo when they were killed back in 1850. Not even Dave Larabee knew about it. That factory would belong to Tom if Larabee was dead. Tom was an invalid now, his wife was dead, and Steve was an only son. Steve would inherit that business when Tom died.

Maybe it had been Steve's fault that there had been a hitch. He'd probably been too cocky because he knew he was going to be rich one day and couldn't wait to spend the money. Tom Gleye had rebelled at covering for his son's big expenses, and the last Steve had talked to him, Tom had threatened to find Dave Larabee and give him the factory in Toledo that was rightfully his. Steve's only chance now to get that factory was to make sure that Dave Larabee was dead. Then there would be nothing that Tom Gleye could do with that factory except leave it to Steve.

The fly in the ointment at the moment was that Pete Cottier had heard enough of the story to know that someday Steve would be rich if Dave Larabee was dead. So he could demand a high price for making sure things worked out that way.

"How about it?" Cottier demanded when Steve was silent too long.

Steve looked at Neff and saw him nod wisely. Steve understood. Once Cottier got rid of Larabee, it wouldn't be too much trouble to dispose of Cottier either through some arranged accident or the vigilantes.

"All right," Steve said. "I'll give you five hundred. But you've got to move fast. Pa threatened to send someone out west to find Dave. If Dave finds out about that factory, he'll head for Toledo in a hurry; then it will be too late to do anything. If you let that happen, you won't get a penny."

Cottier nodded. "That's all right with me. I don't figure on getting paid for something I don't do. I'll get rid of him."

"It will have to be a fair fight or some accident," Neff warned. He looked at Steve. "Maybe we should think of some way to keep this man of your pa's from finding Larabee, just in case Pete bungles it again."

Steve nodded, thinking that maybe Neff's brains would be worth the third of the business Steve had promised him for his help in this scheme. That deal would make Neff a tidy sum and would get Steve completely off the hook for his gambling debt.

"Let's give Pete a chance to do his job first," Steve said. "I've got an idea how we can coax Larabee up here to the hotel. Think you can take care of him if you get him here, Pete?"

"I can take care of him wherever I find him," Cottier said confidently.

"His girl," Neff said, nodding at Steve in approval. "He thinks Brenda is still pining away for him, I suppose."

"No reason for him to think anything else," Steve said. "He doesn't know how much money means to her. Since I've told her I'm going to be rich, I've got the inside track with her."

"Set it up as soon as you can," Neff said. "When is this representative of your pa's coming?"

"I don't know," Steve said. "If Pa knows that Dave planned to sell his hides here in Sheridan, it could be any day now."

"Set that trap no later than tomorrow," Neff said, standing up to indicate that the meeting was over.

Steve frowned. He had called the meeting. But it was Neff who had taken charge. Neff held those gambling debts over his and Cottier's heads to assure him of that power. He reveled in power, and he never missed a chance to flaunt what he had.

Outside Neff's room Steve turned down the hall. He could see a sliver of light coming from under the door of Brenda's room. If she was still up, he might as well set this trap for Larabee right now while he had the courage to attempt it.

His knock brought Brenda to the door. After a moment's surprise she invited him in.

"I thought you'd still be touring the town," she said.

"I decided you might enjoy some company," Steve said. "You never seem to get out of your room much. Have you seen Dave any more?"

Brenda nodded. "Down on the street not an hour ago. You told me he was going to California and would never come back."

"That's what he told me," Steve lied. "He probably figured on using the money from the hides he lost to get to California. Anyway, with him still here, there's a chance that Pa might decide to let him have part of that shoe factory in Toledo. Now you want me to get all of that, don't you?"

Brenda looked sharply at Steve. "I want to live in the city, if that's what you mean."

"That's exactly what I mean. Look at it practically, Brenda. Dave and I could never be partners in anything. If Pa leaves that factory to both of us, we'll have to sell it, and neither one of us will live in Toledo. But if you help me get that, I'll take you there, and we'll live like millionaires."

"Help you?" Brenda exclaimed. "What do you mean?"

"If Dave goes on to California, Pa will cut him out of his will. If you'll invite him up here to your room, a couple of us will corner him and convince him to head west. If we surprise him, there will be no guns used, and nobody will get hurt."

"Maybe Dave won't stay in California."

"Pa ain't going to live long; you know that. When he dies, I'll inherit everything he has. After that, it makes no difference what Dave Larabee does. How about it?"

Steve could see that Brenda didn't like the plan. Maybe she was still in love with Larabee. He was glad he hadn't yielded to his first impulse and laid all his cards on the table. If she knew they intended to kill Larabee, she'd never go along with the plan. But she wanted to live in the city. Steve was banking on that to ensure her help.

"All right," she said finally. "Just so Dave isn't

hurt." She smiled at Steve. "It will be wonderful living in Toledo."

"It sure will," he agreed.

He just hoped she kept thinking of Toledo instead of Larabee when it came time to coax him up to her room.

CHAPTER 5

Larabee worked his way down the street, moving in and out of saloons, which were the only places open now. There were freighters, gamblers, construction workers, buffalo hunters, and even a sprinkling of soldiers. And everywhere there were the women coaxing every unattached man to spend his money at the bar.

Nowhere, though, did Larabee find an overweight buffalo hunter. Among the hunters, he would stand out, Larabee thought, because most of them were thin, wiry men. Larabee could understand that. He'd lost ten pounds on his hunt, mainly, he thought, because food just didn't seem very appetizing when everything smelled of dead carcasses and curing hides. This man Larabee was looking for must have a cast-iron stomach to be able to eat well while on a hunt.

Finally Larabee came to the last of the saloons. There weren't many buildings ahead. There was O'Brien's warehouse, and beyond that the railroad water tank and the livery barn. There was a light in the house behind the warehouse, and Larabee headed for that.

Larabee was surprised to find the entire O'Brien family plus the warehouse clerk, Frank Woods, in the big room of the house.

"Get the job?" Tully asked Larabee as he invited him inside.

Larabee nodded. "I've been looking all over town for the fat hunter. Didn't find anybody who fitted that description."

"If you'd have found him, we'd have dealt with him tonight," Woods said.

Larabee glanced at Tully. "Isn't your meeting over?"

Tully nodded, and when Larabee looked at Mrs. O'Brien and the two girls, Misti and Annie, he explained. "We're waiting for the undertaker to get back. I sent him out after Kelly. He took two men with him."

Mrs. O'Brien set some cups on the table, and Misti brought the coffeepot from the stove. The men gathered around the table. Annie went to the pantry and brought out a glass of milk for herself, then sat up to the table with the others.

"We'll have the funeral tomorrow morning," Tully said. "I made arrangements with the preacher. I hope the undertaker got to the Smoky before dark. Otherwise he might have trouble finding the place."

Larabee nodded. "Could be. There are a lot of gullies running down to the creek. If he didn't find our campsite, he won't know where to look. Our pots and pans were still right where I left them. That should help him."

Misti took the coffeepot back to the stove. When she returned, Woods shifted his chair over beside hers. Larabee assumed that Woods' place beside Misti was an understanding in the family, but he noticed that Annie took exception to that. She scowled over her glass of milk as she watched Woods and her sister. Seeing Annie's frown, Larabee took closer note of Misti. There was no mistaking Woods' intentions, but Larabee saw no response on Misti's part.

Time dragged slowly for those waiting for the undertaker's return. Woods, however, seemed unaware of the gloomy atmosphere. Twice he leaned far over to whisper something to Misti, and each time Annie frowned harder.

"This ain't no courting parlor," she said finally, the words dropping into the wake like rocks in a tin bucket.

Color flooded Misti's cheeks. Woods' face turned red, too, but Larabee thought it was more from anger than embarrassment. Mrs. O'Brien stepped into the lull that followed Annie's words.

"It's long past your bedtime, Annie," she said.

"All right," Annie said, getting off her chair. "But this is no time for him to be making moon eyes at Misti."

"That will do, young lady," Tully said, but the words could have carried more sting, Larabee thought.

Annie left the room, but the embarrassment stayed. It was broken only a minute later by the creak of a wagon outside. Tully hurried to the door.

Larabee stayed inside, but he heard Tully talking to someone outside before he came back in.

"That was the undertaker," he announced when he returned. "He found the camp without any trouble. The funeral will be at ten tomorrow morning." He turned to Larabee. "You can sleep in the warehouse tonight if you'd like."

Larabee nodded. With no money, a debt to Tully, and only the promise of a job, he'd have to sleep somewhere other than at the hotel. The warehouse offered the finest shelter he'd had in over a month.

Mrs. O'Brien brought him a blanket, and he went out the front door and across the open space between the house and the rear of the warehouse. Tully went along and unlocked the door.

"If you didn't lock up everything here at night, you wouldn't have any business next morning," Tully said. "I'll leave the door unlocked, though, with you there. You might get your sleep disturbed."

"I won't worry about that," Larabee said. "It can't be any worse than wondering if Indians are sneaking up on you just waiting for daylight."

"Reckon not," Tully agreed.

Tully went back to the house, and Larabee saw Frank Woods going up the street. He apparently had a room at the hotel or some rooming house. There were several so-called rooming houses in town that were nothing more than huge tents. Some had wooden floors, and others didn't appear to have even that degree of comfort.

The warehouse was half-full of buffalo hides. Larabee took the lantern that Tully had given him and checked the place for intruders before blowing out the light. There were stacks of wolf and coyote hides and also some skunk hides. Their odor clung to them and mingled with the stench of the other hides that weren't completely cured.

At one end of the warehouse were three dozen barrels. Coming close to them, he caught the smell of whiskey, as though one of the barrels might be leaking.

He went back to a bale of coyote hides that seemed to be free of odor. Arranging his blanket, he laid down with the hides for a pillow. The floor of the warehouse was of solid thick planks laid on pilings four feet above the ground. The height of the floor made loading and unloading freight wagons much easier.

He was sure he hadn't been asleep more than half an hour when a noise somewhere at the far end of the warehouse awakened him. He remained quiet, thinking of the night before when the approach of the three raiders had awakened him. But this wasn't the open prairie. The danger here might be as great, but it would be different.

Then he heard the noise again. It sounded to Larabee like tapping on the floor. After a moment, it stopped again. Softly Larabee got out of his blanket, picked up his gun, and moved across the floor toward the sound, pausing occasionally to listen. When the sound was repeated, he realized that it was coming from underneath the floor. Remembering the four-foot pilings the warehouse was sitting on, he reasoned that whatever was making the sounds was underneath the warehouse.

Moving quietly to the door, Larabee eased it open and stepped out on the wooden steps that led down to the ground. When he was far enough down the steps that he could stoop over and look beneath the floor, he stopped and tried to penetrate the darkness under the warehouse. He couldn't see a thing.

Then the sound came again, and this time he pinpointed it. Easing down off the steps, he felt his way among the pilings under the warehouse, keeping stooped over so that his head wouldn't hit the floor.

He was within three feet of the sound when he heard it again. Stopping short, he stared in that direction until he made out the dim figure of a man crouching there.

Larabee gripped his gun. "Hold real still, fellow!" he snapped. "I've got an itchy finger."

Larabee heard a gasp and realized that the other man hadn't known there was anyone near. A minute later when the man spoke, he understood why. His voice was thick and blurred with whiskey.

"Don't shoot, mister. I ain't hurting nothing."

"What are you doing under here?" Larabee demanded.

He realized that was a foolish question, considering the drunken state of the man. He might not even know where he was. Larabee could even smell the whiskey. It was stronger here than it was in some of the bars downtown.

"I ain't hurting nothing," the man repeated.

"Get out from under here," Larabee ordered. "But don't try to slip away."

The man waddled along in a low crouch, and Larabee expected him to spill forward on his face any instant, but he made it out from under the floor of the warehouse without mishap. He stopped there, and Larabee pressed up close to him.

"Who are you?"

"Zeke Quincey," the man said.

Larabee recalled the construction worker who had appeared at the warehouse shortly after the work train had pulled in.

"Don't you have any place to spend the night?"

Quincey was slow in answering. "I was figuring on spending it under the warehouse," he said. "Costs money to sleep in a hotel in this town."

Larabee supposed Quincey had spent all his money on whiskey. "Sleeping under a warehouse like this could cost you a bullet in the guts, too," he said.

Quincey sighed. "I reckon so. You won't tell O'Brien, will you?"

Larabee hesitated. Zeke Quincey wasn't as drunk as Larabee had at first thought. He seemed pretty concerned lest Tully O'Brien find out he had been trying to spend the night under his warehouse. If he'd been as drunk as Larabee had thought, he wouldn't have cared what Tully thought.

"Why shouldn't I tell him?"

"You've never seen that Irish temper of his," Quincey said. "He might kill me. I'll make it worth your while if you won't tell him I sleep under his warehouse."

"You mean you make this a habit?"

"I ain't about to pay the price the hotel asks for a room," Quincey said indignantly.

"Just how will you make it worthwhile for me to keep quiet?" Larabee asked.

"I gathered from what I heard this evening around town that you're looking for information. I get around to a lot of saloons and places where people talk. I hear a lot."

"I thought you worked on the construction crew."

"I do," Quincey said. "But I got assigned to the supply crew. I come in almost every night with the work train to get material we'll need for the next day's work."

"If you get drunk every night, you must not be worth much the next day," Larabee said.

"Oh, I don't get as drunk as you think. You tell me

what you want to know, and I'll listen for it. That is, providing you don't tell Tully O'Brien that I sleep under his warehouse."

Larabee considered the proposition. He couldn't see what harm a half-drunk construction worker could do sleeping under the warehouse. He doubted if Quincey could find out much about the men Larabee was looking for, but he would have on advantage. No one would suspect him of being the ears for Larabee.

"It's a deal," Larabee said. "I want to find the three men who jumped me and my partner, Kelly O'Brien, at our camp on the Smoky Hill. I don't know much about them except that one is a buffalo hunter who is very fat and not too tall."

"Those buffalo hunters come and go pretty fast," Quincey said. "Once they sell their hides and have their spree, they usually head back for more hides. But I'll watch and listen. A hog-fat buffalo hunter shouldn't be too hard to find."

Zeke Quincey scooted back under the warehouse, and Larabee let him go. He went back to his own bunk inside the warehouse. Although he listened, he heard no more sounds under the building, and he decided that Quincey must have settled down to sleep off his whiskey and be ready for another day's work tomorrow.

Tully invited Larabee in to breakfast with the family shortly after sunup, and an hour later the minister came down the street and went over the plans for the funeral with Tully. There was a large tent on the north side of the track where the minister held his church services. The undertaker had already put the body in a casket and had it at the tent church. It wasn't far from the church to the cemetery on the hill north of the town.

Larabee screwed up his courage as ten o'clock approached. He'd rather face a fight than a funeral, especially with three women so directly involved.

Thirty minutes before the time set, a rider came swinging up the street from the west shouting the news that a herd of buffalo had been sighted just northwest of town. Men ran for their horses and heavy rifles. Selling buffalo hides was one of the most profitable businesses in Sheridan, and it wasn't often that the hides came right to town for the hunters.

Horses thundered out of town, some carrying men who were dressed in their best for the funeral. They couldn't afford to take time to change. Once the first hunters arrived at the herd and began shooting, the herd would lumber off, and the latecomer might not get any hides at all.

"We won't think bad of you if you go, too," Tully said. "Hunting buffalo is your job."

"Not this morning," Larabee said. "Besides, this is going to end up in a buffalo stampede and a fight among the men over who killed which buffalo. I'd rather stay out of it."

"Reckon you're right about that," Tully said. "Let's get over to the church."

The seats in the tent, which were simply planks laid across kegs, were only half full. Larabee guessed that the place would have been filled if so many men hadn't gone out on the hunt.

The service wasn't as depressing as Larabee had anticipated. Mrs. O'Brien cried softly through most of it, but the two girls, Misti and Annie, sat almost dry-eyed, staring unseeingly straight ahead.

There wasn't much the minister could say except to eulogize the life of the young boy. Most of his message was directed toward the family, reminding them that they could take comfort in the fact that they need never be ashamed of anything the dead boy had ever done.

Only when the men carried the coffin out of the tent and headed up the hill toward the cemetery did Misti and Annie let the tears break forth.

As the service at the graveside ended, Larabee turned to look down over the town, sprawled out for nearly a mile up and down the track. The river here formed something of an "S," coming in from the west, turning south directly west of town, then swinging to the east again south of town.

A low rumble coming in on the breeze made him turn. He saw nothing, but he recognized the sound to the north and a little to the west. Tully had heard the sound, too, and was staring off toward the hills to the north.

"What is that?"

"Buffalo stampede," Larabee said. "They've got the herd running. Let's get back to town. No telling where those critters will go."

Tully called to his family, and they started down the hill on the run. Their retreat from the cemetery was in sharp contrast to the slow, solemn procession that had climbed the hill a few minutes earlier.

It wasn't until they had reached the bottom of the hill, passing the first of the dugouts that dotted the hillside, that Larabee realized that Annie wasn't with them.

Larabee looked back at the cemetery. The hill was abandoned now; even the men waiting to fill the grave had left their job and were running toward town. Larabee switched his gaze to the northwest. The leaders of the herd were in sight now. Larabee guessed that most of the animals would go west of the town. But then he saw something that made him forget the threat to the town. Annie was over on the far side of the livery stable watching the stampede coming.

"Where's Annie?" Tully yelled, discovering just then that the girl was gone.

Larabee started running, not even taking time to answer. The stampeding animals were charging blindly ahead, completely ignoring the buildings and corrals in their path. Larabee could see some men on horseback behind them and hear the loud booming of the big rifles.

When Larabee reached the livery barn, the leaders of the stampede were only a hundred yards away. Larabee had learned the hard way that a buffalo would rather run over something than go around it if he was either frightened or angry. These animals were both.

Annie was west of the barn, staring at the herd coming over the rise to the northwest. Either she didn't see those animals on her right, or she thought they would turn aside like cattle at sight of her.

Larabee weighed his chances. Annie would get run down where she was, and if he went after her, he would probably get the same. It wasn't much of a choice.

CHAPTER 6

Larabee dashed toward Annie. He heard Tully far behind him, yelling at the top of his voice. He hoped that Tully stayed out of the path of the stampede.

"Annie!" Larabee shouted. "Get back here!"

Annie wheeled to look at Larabee. It was then that she saw the stream of animals coming down the ravine north of the barn. She stared, paralyzed with fear. Her mouth dropped open to scream, but no sound came.

Larabee reached her and grabbed her arm. She came out of her momentary paralysis and started running, almost keeping up with Larabee. He headed back for the barn, not even sure that the barn would turn the lumbering animals, but it was the only place within reach that offered any protection at all.

Larabee dived behind the end of the barn, dragging Annie with him, just as a wild-eyed buffalo bull charged past, not giving an inch to anything in front of him.

Larabee heard the corral fence behind the barn give way under the weight of the big animals. Then the horses that had been in the corral thundered past the east side of the barn, wild-eyed with terror.

Larabee moved nearer the center of the barn as the building quivered under the crash of animals being shoved against the north side by the herd pouring out of the ravine. Mingled with the rumble of the pounding hoofs was the heavy breathing and snorting of the frightened animals. Their red eyes were like coals of fire as they swept past the barn. Foam flicked from their mouths and splashed against the side of the barn. Annie clung to Larabee now, the fear that she had so blatantly ignored earlier making her tremble.

Then they were gone, thundering on past the water tank and splashing across the creek, disappearing toward the main branch of the Smoky Hill. Larabee led Annie, crying now, back up the street toward O'Brien's Warehouse, which had escaped the path of the stampede by only a few yards. The water tank had miraculously withstood the bumpings it had received. The livery barn would have some splintered boards to replace, and the entire corral behind the barn would have to be rebuilt. The owner had stayed inside during the stampede, but now he was in the street demanding that somebody make the hunters who had driven the herd through town get right down there and fix his corral and round up his horses that had run away.

Mrs. O'Brien ran to meet Larabee and Annie and wrapped her daughter in her arms, matching the girl's sobs. Larabee expected Tully to give Annie a rough reprimand for running out to see the stampede when she should have realized the danger. But he seemed too relieved to see her safe to think of correcting her.

Most of the hunters had dropped back when they saw where they were chasing the herd. Now they came riding into town like sneaking pups, by twos and threes, as if expecting the town to meet them with rifles and order them to get out of town and stay out.

But the biggest percent of the town had been spared the trampling that the west end had received. To the inhabitants of this section it had been an exciting episode. It wasn't often that the people who made their living here in town ever saw the live animals responsible for the money they managed to wangle from the hunters.

"There's no way we can thank you," Tully said to Larabee as Mrs. O'Brien and Misti took Annie on to the house.

"You've already done enough for me," Larabee said. "After I saw her, there just wasn't time to ask who wanted to go get her."

"We were extremely fortunate," Tully said. "Annie wasn't hurt, and the herd missed my warehouse and my home."

"I'll figure our luck has really changed when we find the men who raided Kelly and me down on the Smoky Hill," Larabee said. "I'm going to do some more looking. That fat buffalo hunter stayed out of sight last night, but he may be wandering around today."

"I have two men looking for him, you know. We'll find him and when we do, the vigilantes will take care of him."

Larabee worked his way up the street, looking into the saloons but seldom going inside. The crowds were small at this time of day, and a quick look through the door told him there was no one inside fitting the description the liveryman had given him of the fat buffalo hunter.

At the Cross-Tie Saloon, he saw Steve Gleye at the bar, but he ducked back outside before Steve saw him. He didn't want to talk to his cousin now. When he got right down to it, he and Steve had very little in common except having grown up in the same house.

At the front of the saloon Larabee paused, trying to decide what to do next. Frustration nagged at him. He had searched the town two or three times since the livery man had given him the description of the man who had sold him the teams and wagons. Just continuing to look up and down the long street of Sheridan didn't fit his idea of accomplishing anything.

While he was still debating his next move, Brenda Bailey came up from behind him. He whirled in astonishment. He had never seen Brenda in a saloon. Then he realized that she hadn't come from the Cross-Tie but from the alley between the saloon and the hotel.

"Wasn't expecting to see you here," he said.

"I can't stay inside that hotel all the time," Brenda said. "It gets lonesome in there. You're one of the few friends I have in Sheridan."

"You shouldn't have come here," Larabee said. "Why don't you go back? I'll come to Kansas City to see you just as soon as I find those thieves and get the money for my hides."

"You may never get that." She looked up the street where activity was picking up as the day wore on. "When Tom Gleye found out I was coming here, he sent an envelope for me to give you if I saw you. Why don't you come up to my room, and I'll get it for you?"

Larabee agreed, considering Brenda carefully. She seemed much more understanding now than she had yesterday. Maybe she had thought things over and changed her mind. Money meant a lot to Brenda, but now that she had adjusted to the realization that he didn't have any and wasn't liable to get a great deal for some time, maybe she had decided that it wasn't so important.

Just before they stepped up on the hotel porch, Larabee thought he caught a glimpse of some movement at the end of the alley between the saloon and the hotel. But when he stopped to look down the alley, it was empty. He dismissed it quickly, his mind returning to the envelope that Tom Gleye had sent to him.

"What's in that envelope?" he asked.

Brenda shrugged. "I don't know. It's sealed. Maybe just a letter. Tom asked me to give it to you if I saw you."

Larabee thought that she could have given the envelope to him yesterday, but he said nothing. Maybe she just hadn't thought of it then. On the hotel porch, out of the sun, Brenda paused again.

"I hear you got a job with the army," she said.

Larabee nodded, almost surprised that she wasn't scolding him for agreeing to haul freight for the army since it wasn't a high-paying job. Uneasiness touched him. She almost seemed to be stalling now when he was eager to get his hands on that envelope.

Opening the door of the hotel, he held it for her, and she went in slowly. He followed her and moved toward the stairs.

"Where is your room?"

"At the head of the stairs."

She made no move to go up the stairs. "What about that envelope Tom sent me?" he asked impatiently.

She looked up the stairs then at Larabee. "I'll get it. You wait here."

She started toward the stairs, and he followed, touching her arm as she reached the first step. When she turned, he met her gaze squarely.

"You're not a very good actor, Brenda," he said. "Something's wrong. What is it?"

She backed off the step, looking up the stairs. Then she nodded her head just a trifle. "My door up there at the head of the stairs is open just a little bit," she said softly. "I know I closed it when I came out."

"We'd better see what is going on," he said, and started around her.

He was on the second step when she caught his arm. "I don't have anything in my room worth risking a fight for."

"Nobody has a right to go into your room when you're not there," Larabee said, turning back to the steps.

Still she held his arm. As he tried to get free, he saw the door at the top of the stairs suddenly jerk back and a hand with a gun appeared. If there was a face behind the gun, Larabee didn't see it.

Throwing himself backward, he knocked Brenda to one side. The gun fired, the bullet ripping into the floor at the far side of the lobby. If Larabee had stood his ground, he would have stopped that bullet with his chest.

The clerk disappeared like magic behind his desk, and the people in the lobby screamed and dived for safety. A volley of bullets came down the stairs from

Brenda's room as Larabee dodged into the corner beside the stairway, out of sight of the room. Poking his head and arm out into the stairway, he answered the fire with a couple of quick shots. Then he ducked back out of range as more bullets ripped down from above.

Larabee realized it was a stalemate now. He didn't dare show himself, and as long as he stayed out of sight, the gunmen above couldn't get to him without coming out on the stairs. They wouldn't do that. They weren't looking for a fair fight.

Upstairs he heard running feet and poked his head into the stairway again. He was just in time to see the back of a man disappearing down the hallway, apparently toward a rear door and stairs. Most hotels had outside stairs in the back.

He started around the corner to the stairs, but Brenda stopped him. "There was more than one man shooting," she said. "Maybe one of them is still there."

Larabee realized that she could be right. He waited for a minute, then impatience prodded him out of his hiding place again. If there was no one waiting, he was just letting the bushwhackers get away.

Hitting the stairs, he bounded up, his gun cocked. There was no sound or movement ahead. Brenda's door was open, and he leaped inside. The room was empty. Dodging outside again, he ran to the end of the hall and jerked open the door to the landing above the stairway leading down to the alley behind the hotel. The alley was empty. The bushwhackers had likely ducked into a saloon somewhere and were having a drink by now.

Turning back, he met Brenda at the head of the

stairs. She went into her room and jerked open the top drawer of her bureau.

"The envelope Tom Gleye sent to you is gone," she reported dully. "Maybe that was what they were after."

Larabee looked closely at Brenda. She didn't sound very perturbed about the loss. The thought tickled his reasoning that maybe there hadn't been any envelope. But if not, why had she invited him up here? If the whole thing had been planned—

He ruled that out. Brenda had just saved his life by keeping him from blundering into an ambush.

"Have any idea who they might have been?"

Brenda shook her head. "They didn't leave any calling cards."

Larabee had already looked around and concluded that the men left nothing but some empty cartridges. "You sure saved my hide when you noticed that door was open."

"I just happened to remember closing it." She touched his arm. "I didn't want you killed. You came close enough the night your partner was murdered."

Larabee resumed his search through town with renewed vigor. He had begun to doubt that the killers he was looking for were still in Sheridan. But after the ambush attempt in the hotel, he knew they were.

His search was interrupted by the arrival of the train from Topeka and Kansas City. Most of the people in town poured out on the porches and along the track to watch. Larabee stood back out of the way as the unloading began, watching the people along the streets. The train had been in only about ten minutes when Ivan Koonce found him.

"You're supposed to be over there helping load your wagon," he shouted.

Larabee had almost forgotten his freighting job in his desire to catch the men who had ambushed him in the hotel.

"Got some freight for Fort Wallace?" he asked.

"Two big loads of it," Koonce said. "We usually have something for the fort on every train that comes in. This time there's a lot of it."

Larabee found two big army wagons on the other side of the train. Four soldiers were there taking crates off a box car and putting them in the wagons. A Mexican was directing the loading.

"This is Julio Romeriz," Koonce said to Larabee when they reached the wagons. "He's the other freighter. Julio, this is Dave Larabee."

Larabee shook hands with the short, heavy-set Mexican then went to work getting his wagon loaded for the seventeen-mile trip to Fort Wallace. He was glad Romeriz was going along. He wasn't sure he could find the way to the fort. The Mexican apparently had been hauling for the army for some time.

"Do we start out tonight?" Larabee asked when the wagons were loaded.

"We'll have enough trouble in the daylight," Romeriz said, surprising Larabee with his good English. "We'll take the wagons to the army camp for the night and start early in the morning."

The soldiers had brought the extra wagon in for Larabee, but he drove it back. Once there, with the mules taken care of, Romeriz said he would stay with the wagons through the night. Larabee welcomed the chance to get back and talk over the day's happening with Tully O'Brien.

It was supper time when Larabee reached the warehouse. Tully was just closing up to go home. He invited Larabee to come with him.

"The two men I had looking over the town report that they have found nothing," Tully said. "They did locate a fat hunter down in one of the saloons on the south side of the track, but he swore he hadn't been out of town for a week, and the girl with him swore to it, too."

Before supper got under way, the work train came in from the southwest where construction was advancing slowly toward Fort Wallace. Larabee saw Zeke Quincey come over to the warehouse before heading downtown. Larabee guessed that Quincey had something he wanted to leave there before going into the main part of town for his supper.

"Do you see much of Quincey here?" Larabee asked, watching Tully closely.

"Every night. The train was a little late getting in tonight. He usually makes it over before I close. You know, I have a feeling he sleeps some nights under the warehouse. He probably spends all he makes on whiskey and doesn't have enough money for a room, even in one of those tents."

"You don't object?" Larabee asked.

"I wouldn't say I like it," Tully said. "But I know what it's like to be down and out. And Quincey seems like a harmless fellow."

Larabee let it drop. Quincey had been sure he'd be in real trouble if Tully found out he was sleeping under the warehouse. Perhaps it was better if Quincey kept on thinking that. He'd be more careful.

Frank Woods wasn't at the O'Brien table for supper. Annie was talking a steady stream about the happenings of the day, especially the buffalo stampede, until her mother made her hush up. Misti had little to say. Larabee guessed that the funeral was still dominating her mood.

Tully, after Annie had been quieted, seemed to sink into a dark mood. He didn't respond to Mrs. O'Brien's quiet questions, but after the women had started cleaning up the table, he opened up to Larabee.

"Got a gambler named York here in town," he said. "He fleeced a man who came in from Kansas City last week. The man tried to get his money back, and York killed him. We don't need his kind here in Sheridan."

"When did that happen?"

"About an hour ago," Tully said. "Must have been while you were taking your load out to the soldier camp. The town is plenty worked up about it. York is a shady character, anyway. Something will have to be done about him."

Larabee didn't pry into the methods being considered. He was convinced that Tully O'Brien and the barber, Ray Horton, were two of the leaders of the vigilantes. Larabee was glad he wasn't in York's shoes.

CHAPTER 7

Shortly after supper, Larabee went over to the warehouse where he had slept the night before. Tomorrow might be a hard day. Julio Romeriz had hinted that it wasn't an easy trip to Fort Wallace.

Larabee had barely gotten to sleep when he was awakened by the same sound that had roused him the night before. For a while he just lay there, sure that Zeke Quincey was making the noise under the warehouse.

Finally, he got up and went to the door. As soon as he dropped to the ground outside, Quincey called to him.

"That you, buffalo hunter?" he whispered.

"What are you doing under there?" Larabee asked.

"Making my bed," Quincey said softly, coming out to the edge of the building. "Am I being too noisy?"

"Sounded like you were fighting with a hissing bull snake," Larabee said. "Aren't you afraid you'll wake up Tully?"

Quincey nodded, a move that Larabee could barely make out in the darkness. "I am that," he said. "You didn't tell him about me sleeping here, did you?"

"Of course not," Larabee said. "I told you I

wouldn't." He sniffed in disgust. "You're drunk again."

"Not drunk," Quincey objected. "Just comfortably soused. I still know what I'm doing."

"Did you see that fat hunter I'm looking for?"

"Didn't see him," Quincey said, "but I heard about him. He got in a fight down in the Bull Head Saloon. At least, they said he was a big fellow, flabby fat. He must be a tough one. Took three men to keep him from knifing the other guy after he licked him."

"Bull Head Saloon? Does he usually hang out there?"

"Don't know," Quincey said. "But I can find out. Sort of have a nose for things like that."

"They must talk a lot around the saloons where you go. Does this hunter have a couple of fellows with him most of the time? What is his name?"

"I didn't ask too many questions," Quincey admitted slowly. "I heard somebody say he was a fat jasper and he was a hunter. Nobody mentioned his name."

"Why didn't you ask? You were supposed to find out things for me if I didn't say anything to Tully about you sleeping here."

"I'll find out," Quincey said quickly. "I— Well, it just happened that I wasn't too popular at that place right at the time I heard about the fight. I didn't want to attract any attention to myself."

"Mooched one drink too many?"

"Something like that. But I can get information for you."

"Ever see anybody wearing a fancy shirt with pearl buttons like this?" Larabee asked, taking the button from his pocket.

Quincey took the button and held it up where the faint light coming from the town touched it.

"Can't say that I have. But I'll find the mates to this if they're in town. That is, if you'll trust me to take this button with me."

Larabee considered. Zeke Quincey was a hard drinker. He might lose the button, or he might not even think to look for a shirt with buttons that matched it while he was making the rounds, sponging drinks.

On the other hand, he did get all around town, and he had a much better chance of finding the man with that particular shirt than Larabee did. Larabee had looked at that button long enough now that he'd recognize another button like it without having to compare it.

"I'll trust you with it," he said finally. "But bring it back to me tomorrow night. I suppose you'll be sleeping here, won't you?"

"Sure figure on it," Quincey said. "Can't afford the prices in town."

"You'd better bed down now before Tully hears you out here and kicks you out."

Quincey leaned against the warehouse. "Ain't much danger of that. Just remembered. He ain't home tonight."

"What do you mean?"

"Just what I said," Quincey said, the whiskey thickening his words a little. "Surely you know Tully's one of the leaders of the vigilantes."

"I guessed it," Larabee said.

"They're having a trial tonight. Ain't nobody supposed to know about it but the vigilantes. But I found out."

"What's it about?"

"The gambler that killed that Easterner who tried to get his money back."

"If you heard about it, maybe the gambler did, too, and got out of town."

"How's he going to get out?" Quincey said. "And where would he go? This is the jumping-off place. Anyway, you can bet some of the vigilantes were watching him to make sure he didn't skip out. But with Tully gone to that meeting, nobody's going to bother me tonight. I'll try to keep the noise down, though, so you can sleep."

Zeke Quincey ducked low and disappeared between the pilings holding up the floor of the warehouse. Larabee climbed back up on the platform and went inside to his blanket. He heard some more thumping around under the building, but he ignored it and went to sleep.

Larabee was up at dawn the next morning and was out in the street in front of the warehouse when he saw the liveryman coming up the street from the barn, walking rapidly toward the main part of town. Larabee looked that way and saw the activity there as men were hurrying toward the east end of town.

"What's going on?" Larabee asked as the liveryman passed.

"Fellow just told me the vigilantes were busy last night," he said. "I'm going up to see if it's somebody I know."

Larabee frowned, not exactly sure what the man meant. But he followed him up the street toward the east end of town. Over a dozen men were out on the street now, all hurrying to the east.

Larabee had heard of the hanging trestle across the second gully east of town, but it wasn't until he had passed the depot where he could see beyond the machine shop to the second trestle that he fully appreciated the name.

There was a small gully between the depot and the machine shop, but the trestle here wasn't very high. The second gully, east of the machine shop, was deeper and the trestle there was eleven or twelve feet high, making it an ideal place to hang a man. According to what Larabee had heard, the vigilantes had used it many times.

Larabee stopped at the first trestle. He could see all he wanted to see from here. A man was dangling under the tracks of the second trestle swaying gently in the morning breeze. His sightless eyes were staring up at the track above him. Larabee was close enough to see that it was someone he didn't know.

"Who is it?" he asked a man who was coming back from the trestle, walking along the ties over the smaller gully.

"That tinhorn who killed the traveler from Kansas City," the man said carelessly as if it really didn't matter.

"Another job for the undertaker," another man said. "I hear he gets paid pretty well for every carcass he takes off that trestle and buries."

"Who pays him?" Larabee asked.

The man shrugged. "He doesn't ask where the money comes from. I reckon the vigilantes would rather kick in enough to bury their victims than do the job themselves."

Larabee went back down the street to the warehouse just as Mrs. O'Brien sent Annie to tell Larabee that breakfast was ready.

"How many were hanging there this morning?" Annie asked eagerly as she discovered that Larabee was coming from up the street.

"One," Larabee said. "Has there been more sometimes?"

"Sure," Annie said excitedly. "Sometimes there are so many there ain't room for them all on the trestle."

"Annie!" Tully said sharply from the doorway. "Be quiet!" He looked at Larabee. "She's got an imagination that would shame a drunk."

"This a common occurrence?" Larabee asked as he came to the table.

"If you're talking about her imagination, it is."

"That wasn't what I meant," Larabee said.

"These other things happen occasionally," Tully said. "Never when it isn't necessary. Pass the bread."

Larabee could see that the subject was closed. Mrs. O'Brien and Misti had nothing to say about it, and Annie had been thoroughly squelched by her father.

"By the way," Tully said when breakfast was half over, "I picked up a letter for you at the post office. Came in on yesterday's train. There was such a hubbub last night over that cold-blooded murder that I forgot to give it to you."

Tully fished a letter out of his pocket and handed it across the table to Larabee. Larabee took it, seeing that it had come from Kansas City.

"I wasn't expecting anybody to write to me," Larabee said, hurrying along with his breakfast.

"Who would know you planned to be here?" Tully asked.

"Tom Gleye, the man who gave me a home after

my parents were killed," Larabee said. "He knew I was going on this hunt and that I hoped to sell my hides here in Sheridan."

In his letter Tom asked Larabee to write to him, telling him where he could be found. Tom wanted to send a man out with something important for Larabee. The letter didn't elaborate, and Larabee could only guess what important thing Tom Gleye could be sending to him. Tom wrote a short letter in reply, telling Tom Gleye that he expected to be in Sheridan for some time now since his load of hides had been stolen and he had been forced to take a job freighting for the army.

Before he had finished addressing the envelope, Ivan Koonce rode up from the army camp outside town.

"You don't keep the army waiting," Koonce said. "Romeriz is ready to go."

"I had a letter I had to answer," Larabee said. He handed the envelope to Tully. "Will you mail this for me?"

"That I will," Tully said. "I've got some mail to send to Kansas City myself."

Larabee found that Koonce had brought along an extra horse, apparently to get Larabee to the camp faster. At the soldier camp, he found none of the urgency that Ivan Koonce had indicated back at O'Brien's. The freighting teams were not even harnessed yet. Larabee guessed that Koonce thought Larabee should be here to harness his own mules.

"Looks like you may have an exciting trip," one soldier said to Larabee as he helped him hitch up the mules.

"What's going to be so exciting about it?" Larabee asked.

"We've been hearing there are several small bands of Indians around close. Could be you'll run into one of them between here and Fort Wallace."

Larabee frowned. "What is the army going to do about it?"

The soldier grinned. "Hope you get through, I reckon." Then his face sobered. "The lieutenant is sending along an escort. Only four soldiers, though."

"Doesn't sound like the army cares much whether we get through or not," Larabee said.

"We ain't got many men here, you'll notice," the soldier said.

With the teams hitched up, Larabee and Julio Romeriz climbed up to the seats of the freight wagons. Romeriz led the way out of the camp, Larabee following. Before they had gone a hundred yards, four soldiers galloped out from the horse corral to overtake them. Larabee saw that Ivan Koonce was one of the four.

Romeriz headed his team down the gully past the livery barn, which looked something like an abandoned trash heap after yesterday's stampede, then around the south side of the twin buttes. There the road turned west until it came within sight of the track that pointed west southwest.

Romeriz twisted around in his seat and yelled above the grind of the wheels and the squeak of the harness, "Stay close to me."

Larabee nodded, understanding Romeriz's concern. If the Indians did strike, he didn't want to be cut off from either the other wagon or the escort of soldiers.

The town had disappeared behind the twin buttes that Annie had called Rattlesnake Hill. Ahead, the railroad track, which came through a cut around the north side of the buttes, stretched out to the horizon. It wasn't long until the work camp came in sight. Close by was the crew, including the gaugers and spikers, nailing the rails to the ties. A few yards ahead the ties were being laid.

"Can't leave any loose ties out here over night," one of the soldiers riding beside Larabee said. "The redskins will drag them off and burn them."

The graders were not too far beyond the other crews. Only stakes marked the survey across the prairie ahead. Larabee wondered if those stakes were ever moved by the Indians and guessed that the line was probably resurveyed just before the grading was done.

Once Larabee saw riders in the low hills off to his right. They were too far away to identify, but they didn't look like Indians. He couldn't imagine what white men would be doing out there.

"Did you see those riders?" Larabee asked Koonce who was riding beside his wagon now.

The soldier nodded. "I saw them."

"They're not Indians."

"That's right," Koonce said. "They may be even more dangerous to us. There are a lot of bandits roaming around just outside town, stealing hides and cargoes. If that's what they've got in mind, they're going to get fooled. Didn't look like more than half a dozen of them."

"Is there anything in these wagons that they'd want to steal?" Larabee asked.

"Ammunition," Koonce said. "Several civilians have Spencers and Henrys."

"If Romeriz and I were alone, we'd be in trouble," Larabee said.

"You would be for a fact," Koonce agreed. He twisted around in the saddle and scanned the prairie in all directions. "You could be, anyway. There may be others. Hard to say."

Larabee kept his wagon close to Romeriz's outfit. Like Koonce, he kept scanning the horizons. Suddenly Koonce stood in his stirrups and pointed ahead and to the right. "There they are!" he shouted. "Pull the wagons together."

Romeriz stopped his wagon, and Larabee whipped his team up beside him. He saw the four riders coming toward the wagons, but they didn't look to Larabee like men on the attack. They were leaning forward in their saddles and whipping their horses furiously.

Then he saw the reason. A half mile behind the four men was a band of almost naked riders.

"Indians!" Koonce screamed. "Get ready to fight."

The soldiers quickly dismounted and led their horses between the two big wagons. Romeriz was assigned to watch the two freighting teams and the soldiers' horses while Larabee joined the soldiers in preparing for battle.

By the time they were ready at the corners of the wagons with their rifles, the four fleeing riders were within a hundred yards. Larabee was glad he hadn't pulled any closer to the other freight wagon when the new riders crowded their horses in between the wagons, too. The puffing horses excited the others, and it took one of the newcomers to help hold them.

Larabee had been watching the approaching Indians, trying to determine how many there were and had barely glanced at the fleeing men. Now that they were dismounting, he turned to look them over and determine how much actual help they would be in fighting off the Indians. The two men closest to him were big fellows, one a Negro. Both were buffalo hunters, judging from their garb.

When men and horses shifted so Larabee could see the other two, his eyes popped. He certainly hadn't expected to see Steve Gleye out here on the prairies. Even more surprising was Slip Neff. The gambler looked as much out of place in this situation as one of those hunters would have been dealing in a saloon.

"What happened?" Koonce demanded.

"We were scouting for buffalo," Neff explained. "Thought some might have been wounded in that chase yesterday and we could take a few hides easy. Bumped into those redskins over yonder."

"So you brought them down on us," Koonce said disgustedly.

"We remembered seeing you army boys. Figured it was our only chance to keep from being scalped."

"Maybe," Koonce said. "Maybe you just furnished them with some more scalps. Everybody get ready. Don't fire till I give the command."

Larabee slid under a wagon and poked his rifle between the spokes of a wheel. There were more than a dozen Indians. Koonce might be right; the Indians could get ten scalps instead of four.

CHAPTER 8

Larabee couldn't get a count on the Indians as they charged toward the wagons, but he was sure they substantially outnumbered the defenders.

Even before the corporal gave the order to fire, the Indians split into two columns and swung in a big circle around the two wagons, one column riding each way. Apparently, sight of the blue uniforms had dampened the enthusiasm of the red warriors. Until they could be sure there weren't too many soldiers, there would be no reckless charge.

As soon as the two columns separated to circle the wagons, all semblance of order disappeared, each rider coming as close to the wagons as his own bravery dictated.

Bullets thudded into the wagons, and one ricocheted off a spoke only inches from Larabee's face. He flopped over involuntarily, then ran a hand over his face to make sure no splinters had lodged there. Grabbing his rifle, he took aim again at a wildly riding Indian and fired.

The range was too long for anything but a lucky shot to score. Apparently the little band of Indians had no stomach for a close encounter with the defenders at the wagons, especially those in blue uniforms.

It was a chance shot that struck the black hunter in the thigh. He swore a little, but didn't even leave his post.

"Take careful aim," Koonce shouted. "If we can pick off one or two of them, they may give up. They don't seem much set on getting our scalps."

The firing stopped as each man picked a target and took deliberate aim. The ragged volley that erupted from the wagons brought down one horse and knocked an Indian off another pony. Larabee had been aiming at that brave, but he wasn't sure he was the only one because that warrior seemed a little more impudent than the others.

Two other braves swooped down, picked up the fallen warrior, and carried him back to safety. The other Indians gathered around them, out of range of the rifles at the wagons. The silence that fell over the prairie was oppressive. No one at the wagons said a word as all eyes focused on the knot of Indians on the ridge to the north.

Judging from the arms waving in the air, Larabee guessed the warriors were having an argument about their next move. After a few minutes the huddle broke up, and the Indians lined out to the northwest at a steady jog.

"Guess that's over," Koonce said with a sigh. He turned to the Negro hunter. "How's that leg?"

"I can get back to town to the sawbones all right," the hunter said.

Larabee looked after the departing Indians, thinking that the fight would certainly have ended differently if there hadn't been soldiers at the wagons or if there had been a few more braves.

Larabee leaned his rifle against the wheel of his

wagon and took his first really good look at the four men who had brought the Indians down on the wagons. He had recognized Steve and Slip Neff, but the two buffalo hunters were men he had never seen before. Both were huge men, looking as if they were capable of strangling a buffalo with their bare hands.

Larabee thought of the fat buffalo hunter who had sold his teams and wagons to the livery man. But he wouldn't call either of these men hog fat. They were just big. And he was sure that the liveryman would have made a point of it if the man he had bought the teams from had been a Negro. So that eliminated one. He might have questioned the other man if he'd found him in a saloon in Sheridan. But the man he was looking for certainly wouldn't be riding with Steve Gleye.

"Just what were you and Neff doing out here this morning?" Larabee demanded of Steve.

"Hunting buffalo like we said," Steve replied. "With all that shooting yesterday, some animals were bound to be wounded. We thought we might pick up some easy hides."

"Any wounded ones were finished off yesterday by all those hunters who were out," Julio Romeriz said, climbing to the seat of his wagon. "The rest of the herd moved on. If you'd stayed in town, we wouldn't have had this trouble."

"You didn't get hurt," the white hunter snapped. "What are you crying about?"

Larabee scowled at the big man. The Negro, who had been wounded, hadn't said a word, but the other hunter sounded as belligerent as an aggravated bull.

"Who is he?" Larabee demanded softly, turning to Steve.

Steve shrugged. "Just a hunter. Name is Pete Cottier."

"It wasn't your fault we didn't get our scalps lifted," Romeriz said.

Cottier took two swift strides to the front wheel of Romeriz's wagon. "You greasy-faced mule skinner!" he shouted. "Don't you get sassy with me!"

Romeriz grabbed his whip and stood up, glaring down at Cottier. "I'll get as sassy as I want to."

Larabee thought the hunter was going to reach for the gun at his hip. But he saw Romeriz cock his arm and realized that the freighter was probably faster with his whip than the hunter was with his gun. Cottier apparently reasoned the same, for he backed off with some choice epithets aimed at the Mexican and his ancestors.

Corporal Koonce helped get the Negro hunter on his horse and saw the four ride off toward Sheridan; then he turned to those left. "Let's get on to Fort Wallace before that bunch of redskins finds some reinforcements and comes back."

Fort Wallace was on Pond Creek close to where it ran into the Smoky Hill. When Larabee got to the fort and discovered the strength of the force there, his confidence dipped. Three companies of infantry and two troops of cavalry, totaling less than two hundred men, under the command of Lt. Col. Charles Woods of the Fifth Infantry, made up the strength of the fort. No wonder there were so few soldiers at Sheridan and the lieutenant there could afford only four men to send as an escort for the freight wagons.

Corporal Koonce and the three privates who had come over from Sheridan with the wagons returned with them. They started from Fort Wallace shortly after sunup the next morning and were within five miles of the town by mid-forenoon.

It was here where the trail paralleled a ravine some distance away that a rifle opened up. The first bullet snapped past Larabee, a clean miss, but he knew it had been close. Larabee dived off the seat, dropping below the level of the high wagon box. The next shot grazed one of the mules, which began to buck. The sniper seemed to be trying to make the mule team run now.

He might easily have succeeded if his fourth shot, apparently aimed at grazing one of the lead mules, hadn't gone astray and killed the mule. With one of the leaders down in the harness, the other mules simply milled around, tangling and breaking harness but not running.

Before that fourth shot had been fired, the soldiers, under Koonce's command, charged away from the wagons toward the ravine. It could have been their charge that had hurried the rifleman's shot and caused him to kill the mule.

The man suddenly left the ravine on a long-legged roan horse. The soldiers opened fire but missed their fleeing target. The speedy roan proved to be more than a match for the army horses, and the rider soon disappeared to the south.

It took half an hour to untangle the mules and patch up the harness so they could move on. Larabee and Romeriz did the work while the soldiers stood watch, rifles ready, in case the sniper returned. Larabee tied the teammate of the mule that had been killed to the tailgate of the wagon and let the other two mules pull the empty wagon on to town.

Larabee said nothing to Romeriz about his conclusions, but he was certain that he had been the sole target of this attack. The first shot had been aimed at him. Only when he disappeared below the level of the wagon box did the attack switch to the mules in an attempt to make them run away.

Larabee turned his outfit over to some soldiers when he arrived at the soldier camp and reported to the lieutenant what had happened. Then he headed for town.

Before he reached O'Brien's Warehouse, he passed several men who were obviously patroling a segment of a rough circle around town. Every man had a gun strapped around his waist and was carrying a rifle.

At the warehouse, he found Frank Woods working on some books in his office, a rifle leaning against the wall just behind him. Even Tully O'Brien had a rifle propped against the wall only a foot from the door.

"What's the idea of all the rifles?" Larabee asked Tully. "The whole town looks like an armed camp."

"It is," Tully said. "Steve Gleye and that gambler, Slip Neff, rode in yesterday with a wounded man. They said the Indians attacked them."

"And you're expecting them to swoop down on the town?" Larabee asked.

"We're going to be ready in case they do."

"Didn't they tell you there were only about a dozen Indians?"

"I didn't hear their story firsthand," Tully said. "But I gathered from what I did hear that there must have been at least two hundred."

Larabee nodded. "Even two hundred would hardly tackle a town this size. What about the workers at the construction camp? Did they all pull back into town?"

"No," Tully said. "If they want to get scalped, that's their business."

"Find out any more about the men who killed Kelly?"

Tully shook his head. "Not a thing. The biggest buffalo hunter I've seen is that one who rode in with Gleye and Neff. Even he doesn't quite fit the description we've been given. Are you going to be around for a while?"

"I figure on it," Larabee said.

"Will you watch things for me? I've got some business up the street."

Shortly after Tully disappeared, Misti and Annie came in. Woods appeared at the door of his little office and motioned Misti inside. Annie followed her. Larabee heard Annie's sharp voice and Woods' angry reply, but he tried to ignore them. That argument was none of his business. Then Annie came charging out of the office with Woods and Misti behind her and came straight to Larabee.

"I wish you'd punch him in the nose!" she snapped.

"Now what has he done to deserve that?" Larabee asked cautiously.

"He's been pawing over Misti like an old tomcat."

"Annie!" Misti exclaimed, her face reddening.

"Well, it's so," Annie insisted, "and I don't like it."

Woods, fighting to control his anger, moved toward Annie. "Annie," he said softly, "if you want me to show you some rattlesnakes, you're going to have to watch your tongue."

"When will you show me some?" Annie asked, her animosity suddenly gone. "Right now?"

"Not with the Indians on the prowl like they are," Woods said.

"There ain't no Indians around now," Annie said disgustedly. "Is there, Dave?"

"We didn't see any coming home from Fort Wallace," Larabee admitted reluctantly.

Annie turned to Woods triumphantly, and Misti took advantage of Woods' distraction to slip out of the warehouse and run back to the house. Larabee watched her go, thinking that this little episode was finished. He saw Annie leave and go to the barn behind the house; shortly after, Woods left, also heading toward the barn.

Larabee frowned. If Tully hadn't left him to watch the warehouse, he'd go see what Woods was up to. Then he heard a buggy beyond the house, but he didn't see it until it was well down toward the river. He couldn't see who was in the buggy because the top was up. In a few minutes a horse galloped after the buggy and Larabee recognized Misti as the rider.

He stood in the doorway and watched as Misti tried to overtake the buggy. But the buggy reached the foot of the buttes first, and Woods and Annie got out. Larabee realized then that Woods was taking Annie into the rocks to show her some rattlesnakes. A foolish move if ever he'd seen one. It was a warm day. The snakes would likely be out sunning themselves. They'd be extremely dangerous if disturbed.

Seeing Tully coming down the street, Larabee felt relieved of his obligation to watch the warehouse, and he leaped down the steps and ran to the barn. Tully's big sorrel was still there, and he lost only a few seconds throwing the saddle on him. Evidently Misti had gone to bring Annie back, but Larabee doubted if Misti could control either Woods or her sister.

Sending the sorrel at a hard gallop, Larabee splashed across the ford and put him up the slope to the foot of the buttes. The buggy was standing at the edge of the dark rocks on the north east side of the buttes, and Woods was guiding Annie up into the rocks. Misti had tied her horse to the buggy wheel and was going after them.

As Larabee dismounted, he saw Misti turn and start back to her horse, Woods after her. Annie stayed, searching through the rocks for snakes. Larabee ran to meet Misti, but she swept past him, anger and fear in her face. He didn't even ask her what was wrong but pushed on to block Woods' path.

"What do you think you're doing?" he demanded, catching Woods by the arm.

Woods wheeled on Larabee. "None of your business!" he shouted, and swung a fist.

Larabee ducked, taking the blow on his shoulder. His own fist smashed into the clerk's stomach, driving the wind out of him. Woods stumbled back and lost his footing on the steep slope. Going down, he started rolling. It was the larger rocks at the foot of the slope that stopped him rather than his own efforts.

Larabee bounded down the slope and was waiting when Woods staggered to his feet. The fury in the clerk's face suddenly drained away as he looked at Larabee, eager to continue the fight.

"You won't be cocky long," Woods said, trying to save some face. "You'll be dead before you see many more sunrises."

Larabee grabbed Woods by the shift front and jerked him up close. "What do you mean by that?"

Woods pinched his lips together, the anger in his face turning to fear. Before Larabee could force an answer from him, a scream up on the slope checked him.

"It's Annie!" Misti screamed. "She must have been bitten by a rattler."

CHAPTER 9

Ignoring Woods, Larabee bounded up the slope with Misti close behind him. Annie was running toward them.

Larabee reached the girl and caught her arm, stopping her. She was holding her right hand over her left wrist. Larabee lifted her hand and saw the two tiny prick marks.

"Sit down," he said calmly.

"I've got to get home," Annie screamed.

"Sit down and be quiet," Larabee said sternly. "We'll take you home as soon as we can."

Misti reached them then, and she sat Annie down on a rock. "What can we do?" she asked, looking at Larabee with tears in her eyes.

Larabee already had his pocket knife out. "I'll lance the spot and try to get some of the poison out. Then we'll take her in to the doc."

Woods had stayed by the buggy. Now he yelled up at them, "Need any help, Misti?"

"Ride in and find the doc and make sure he's in his office," Misti called back. "We'll bring Annie in."

Woods took the sorrel Larabee had ridden out and put him to a gallop toward town.

Larabee squeezed Annie's arm tightly above the pricks then quickly made a short slash across her wrist, hitting both of the tiny holes. Annie screamed as the knife cut through the skin, but then she gritted her teeth and made no other sound except for her sobs.

Larabee sucked the blood that welled up from the cut he had made, spitting it out quickly. He repeated this a few times then took the neckerchief from around his neck and wrapped it tightly around Annie's arm above the wound.

"Let's go," Misti said.

"I'll carry Annie," Larabee said.

"I can walk," Annie said stoutly.

"Of course you can," Larabee said. "But I don't want you to. I heard a doc say once that anybody bitten by a rattler shouldn't exercise any more than was necessary."

Stooping, he picked up the girl and started down the slope. Misti ran on ahead and untied her pony from the wheel of the buggy and retied the reins to the back where he could be led to town. By then, Larabee had reached the buggy, and Misti helped get Annie into the back seat where she sat and held her sister's head in her lap. Larabee got in the front and picked up the reins.

Whipping the team into a run, he headed for town, the pony behind pulling back hard on its reins until it understood it had to run to keep up. They hit the ford in the creek and splashed water high as they charged across. The water wasn't deep or wide here, and Larabee guessed that in the dry season it might not be running at all.

Larabee passed the water tank and O'Brien's Warehouse without even pausing. In front of the general store, he jerked the team to a stop. People quickly began to crowd around, attracted by the sight of the buggy racing up the street. Larabee lifted Annie from the buggy and pushed through the crowd without answering the questions thrown at him.

As he climbed the outside steps to the doctor's office, he heard Misti telling someone that Annie had been bitten by a rattler and asking them to tell her parents.

Woods was in the doctor's office when Larabee pushed the door open. Dr. Epstein was taking some medicine from his shelves. Larabee laid Annie on the couch in the office and stepped back, letting the doctor take over.

The doctor worked calmly as if this were an everyday occurrence. Larabee didn't pay much attention to what he did. He probably wouldn't have understood it if he had watched.

"You did a good job in getting this to bleed," the doctor said as he worked. "A lot of the poison came out with the blood."

"Will she be all right?" Misti asked anxiously.

"Of course she will," the doctor said positively, and Larabee wondered if he was really as confident as he sounded. "Annie's a stout little girl. But she should know better than to go up on the buttes. There are a lot of rattlers up there."

Larabee knew that last was meant to be a warning to Annie. But he doubted if she needed it now. She had finally seen a snake, and it wasn't likely that she would want to see another one right away.

Woods went down the stairs and took the horse he had ridden into town back to the barn behind the warehouse. Tully O'Brien and his wife arrived in the doctor's office a couple of minutes later.

The doctor eased the concern of the parents; then Mrs. O'Brien asked if they could take Annie home.

"Of course," the doctor said. "I think you'd better carry her, Tully. I want her kept as quiet as possible."

Tully carried Annie down the stairs followed by Mrs. O'Brien. Larabee came behind with Misti.

"You'll have supper with us, won't you, Dave?" Misti asked as they came to the street.

"You'll have enough confusion there tonight without me," he said.

"I want you to come," she said.

He looked squarely at her. Glints from the late afternoon sun were reflecting from her reddish blonde hair, and her sky-blue eyes had an earnest appeal in them that he found hard to refuse. He supposed she was trying to thank him for what he had done. He didn't want any thanks, but refusing an invitation to supper was not the way to tell her so.

"I'll be there," he said.

Tully had put Annie in the buggy, and now he drove it slowly down the street to the warehouse and around behind it to the house. Larabee walked with Misti behind the buggy. A man was standing on the platform in front of the warehouse looking at the people coming along the street. When he saw Misti and Larabee, he came down the steps and stopped them.

"Are you Dave Larabee?" he asked.

Larabee nodded.

"I've got a telegram for you. Came in just a few minutes ago. The depot agent said I might find you here at O'Brien's."

Larabee took the telegram and flipped it open. It

was from Tom Gleye in Kansas City. He was surprised that Tom had even had time to get his letter. Then he remembered that he had sent that letter the morning before he took the load of freight to Fort Wallace. A lot had happened since then.

"Am sending Clyde Voss to Sheridan to talk to you," the telegram said, and it was signed Tom Gleye.

"Not bad news, I hope," Misti said.

Larabee shook his head. "Not much news at all. My uncle is sending a man to talk to me. He didn't say what about. Uncle Tom was always close-mouthed, but this takes the cake. All I know about this man Voss is that he's a lawyer."

"When is he coming?"

Larabee shrugged. "Uncle Tom didn't say that."

"I'm going to go in and start supper," Misti said. "I'll call when it's ready."

Larabee went to the front of the house where Tully had left the buggy with the team still hitched to it and Misti's pony tied to the back. He put the horses in the barn and took care of them; then he went back to the warehouse.

Zeke Quincey was there, slouched down by the steps at the front of the warehouse. He had evidently just come from the main part of town. He wasn't drunk yet, but he had been drinking.

"Have you found the shirt with the missing button yet?" Larabee asked, stopping and looking down at Quincey.

Quincey got to his feet, a trifle unsteadily. "I found it, all right."

"Who does it belong to?"

"Now you didn't think I was going to get myself

killed just to find that out, did you? I saw the shirt in a room at the hotel, but I don't know who it belongs to."

Larabee nodded. "Never mind. If you'll tell me what room it is, I'll find out for myself."

"I can show you," Quincey said. "But we'd better wait till after supper. Most of the people in the hotel go to the saloons then to do some drinking and make a lot of noise, so we shouldn't be bothered."

Larabee thought of the supper Misti was getting for him. He didn't want to miss that.

"I'll meet you here right after I eat," Larabee said.

Quincey nodded. "I'll be here. Better take this button, too. I've been afraid I'd lose it, and I figured you'd break my neck if I did."

"You figured right," Larabee said, taking the button and putting it in his pocket.

Quincey scooted down against the steps again, and Larabee went on inside the warehouse. Impatience gnawed at him. He thought of going over to the house where Tully had stayed, evidently too concerned about Annie to come back to the warehouse, and tell him what Quincey had said. Tully was vitally concerned about that. But it would be better, he decided, to wait until he found the man instead of just the shirt. Tully had enough on his mind right now.

Frank Woods stayed in the little office, apparently working on the books, until Misti came over and said that supper was ready. There had been no customers at the warehouse in the half hour Larabee had been waiting. Woods closed up the warehouse and went over to O'Brien's with Larabee. Larabee guessed that Woods ate at O'Brien's most of the time.

When Woods discovered that Larabee was going to O'Brien's for supper, too, his displeasure was apparent. But that displeasure was quickly drowned by the wave of coolness that hit him when he got inside. It was obvious that Tully felt that Woods was mostly responsible for Annie's being bitten by that rattler.

It was a good supper, and Larabee managed a minute alone with Misti to tell her so. Then he hurried back to the warehouse. He found Quincey close to the back door waiting for him.

"Figured you'd be champing at the bit," Quincey said. He glanced up at the darkening sky and at the lights winking on over town. "Reckon supper is about over at the hotel. We won't go in till they all clear out."

Quincey insisted on stopping at the Cross-Tie Saloon to make sure that some of the men he knew stayed at the hotel were there. If they weren't, it was too early to go to the hotel. Larabee thought it was just an excuse for Quincey to get to the bar where he could get another drink.

After one drink, however, Quincey pushed away from the bar and headed for the door, nodding to Larabee. "Supper's over," he said softly.

"What were you doing in the hotel when you saw the shirt?" Larabee asked as they left the saloon.

"I had some business there," Quincey said, turning down the alley between the saloon and the hotel. "We'll go in the back way. No use explaining to the clerk what we're up to."

Larabee followed Quincey up the back stairs. Quincey moved silently now, and Larabee matched his caution as they headed for a room at the far end of the hall. Quincey stopped once when a man stepped out of a room and caught his arm.

"When are you going to bring more goods?" he asked.

Larabee saw that the man was drunk, his eyes watering and his voice thick. He was holding on to Quincey's arm partly to keep Quincey from going on down the hall and partly to keep from falling down himself.

"I'll let you know," Quincey said shortly, and jerked away.

The man stared after Quincey, swearing softly. Then, after glaring at Larabee as though he were an intruder, he staggered back into his room and slammed the door.

Larabee frowned as he looked from the closed door to Quincey. There was something here that needed explaining. Did Quincey's business here at the hotel have something to do with this man? The only thing a man like that would likely be interested in was more to drink.

Larabee put it from his mind. He had more important things to do here in the hotel. Once he found the shirt with the missing button, he was sure he could find the man who owned it.

Quincey suddenly stopped just ahead of Larabee. "This is the room," he whispered.

Larabee looked at the door. It was closed, and there was no light coming from under it. The dim light in the hallway barely showed him the number, 23.

"Suppose we can get in?" Larabee whispered.

"Sure. The locks ain't much good in this hotel."

Quincey reached out and pushed the door. It wasn't even latched, but the hinges protested loudly as it swung open.

Once inside, Larabee closed the door, trying to ignore the squeaking hinges, then reached into his pocket for a match. Striking the match, he located the lamp, then lit it.

"There it is," Quincey whispered, pointing to a bundle of clothes in the corner of the room. "That's it, ain't it?"

Larabee picked up the silk shirt, then nodded. "It sure is. Who stays in this room?"

"I don't know," Quincey said. "I didn't want to get snoopy enough to get my head blown off."

"You did what I asked you to," Larabee said. "If I look around, I should find something to tell me who is staying here."

Larabee went to the bureau and pulled out a drawer. Before he had time to see what was inside, a heavy footstep sounded out in the hall as someone hit the top of the stairs.

"Somebody's coming," Quincey whispered in alarm.

Larabee reached over and blew out the light. The next instant the door burst open. In the sudden darkness after the lamp went out, Larabee couldn't see anything.

"Break into my room, will you?" a man yelled.

The next instant Larabee was hit by a charging body that sent him reeling across the room. He was aware that another man was coming into the room, too, but he had his hands full with the first man. Let Quincey take care of the other one.

He swung a fist at the moving hulk in front of him. The fist connected, but he took a hard jolt to the side of his head in return. Suddenly he was aware that the second man was moving in on him, too. Apparently Quincey had kept quiet until he could slip past the men out of the room.

Larabee felt that he could handle one man. But two boring in on him in the dark promised to be more than he could manage. He couldn't tell much about the men except that one was as big as he was and the other one smaller. But the little man's fists stung plenty when they landed.

One thought kept Larabee fighting doggedly. One of these men was the owner of that shirt. He was the man who had stolen his loads of hides. Larabee had been looking for him for a long while, and now he was in the same room with him.

Two more hard blows to his head, however, made Larabee reconsider his good fortune in finding the man he wanted. He realized that he was going to be lucky to get out of this alive. They would kill him if they could. They had tried out on the Smoky Hill. They wouldn't miss a second time if they could help it.

A hard blow to the stomach doubled Larabee over. In that position, he drove toward the door with all the power his legs could muster. If he didn't get out of this room in another minute, he knew he would never get out.

He hit the little man in the stomach and sent him reeling. The bigger man lunged at him and missed. Then Larabee was through the door and darting down the hall toward the back door, which Quincey was holding open. He went down the steps three at a time with Quincey at his heels.

He realized he'd been very lucky to get out of that hotel alive.

CHAPTER 10

Dodging around the corner of the Cross-Tie Saloon, Larabee led the way into the activity that flowed up and down the busy main street. At O'Brien's Warehouse, Zeke Quincey quickly disappeared underneath the building where he would spend the night. Larabee, however, wasn't satisfied to call it a day. He had come so close to identifying the men who had robbed him and killed his partner that he couldn't rest without making another effort to complete the job.

Larabee hesitated about going back to the hotel where the men who had jumped Quincey and him might still be waiting. But his only chance to get the name of the man who had lost the shirt button down on the Smoky Hill was to find out who had rented Room 23 in the hotel.

He reached into his pocket for the telegram from Tom Gleye to read it again. But it was gone. He must have lost it during the scuffle in the hotel room. He shrugged. He remembered everything the telegram said, anyway.

There was a light in the front of the hotel, but when he stepped into the lobby, he saw that the clerk was gone. He slapped his hand on the little bell on the desk, but nobody responded.

He thought of going upstairs and looking in Room 23, but he ruled that out quickly. It would be a perfect ambush. Whoever had rented that room very likely had stayed there after Larabee and Quincey had left.

Turning the register around, Larabee studied it. There was no one listed in Room 23 at all. Puzzled, Larabee turned the pages back. A Herman Brown was the last name registered in that room, and he had checked out a week ago. There had been someone in there tonight. Something funny was going on.

Larabee looked longingly at the stairs again, then turned and went back outside instead. Tomorrow morning when the clerk was on duty, he'd get some answers.

It was quiet underneath the warehouse when Larabee climbed the steps to his blankets. Evidently Quincey was asleep. Once during the night, he heard some movement under the floor, but he ignored it and went back to sleep.

As soon as he had had breakfast, Larabee headed up the street again to the hotel. The clerk was behind the desk this morning, and Larabee came to the point immediately.

"Who is staying in Room 23?"

The clerk's face turned a shade whiter, it seemed to Larabee, and he didn't answer for a moment. He looked at the register as though studying it for the first time in his life.

"There is nobody in 23," he said. "Would you like to register for it?"

"There was somebody in it last night," Larabee said. "I just want to know who it was."

The clerk looked at the register again. "That room was empty last night."

Larabee looked the clerk in the eye. "That's a lie, and you know it."

The clerk dropped his gaze. "People are checking in and out all the time."

"Where are they going? There is no way out of town except when the train goes back East or the stage goes west to Denver. Neither one has left since last night. Give me the straight of it, or I'll gun whip you."

Larabee leaned over the desk, and the clerk backed off, fear in his eyes. "There's nobody in that room, mister," he said. "Go up and see for yourself."

"I'll just do that," Larabee said.

He took the steps two at a time and turned down the hall toward 23. He was already sure he'd find nobody there now. The clerk had been too positive. But the clerk had to know who had been there and where he had gone.

The room was empty, but the bed was rumpled just like Larabee recalled seeing it last night. Whoever had been in this room had cleared it out as soon as Quincey and Larabee had left last night. Larabee decided to watch both the train and the stage on their next trips out of town. He'd have some questions to ask anyone coming from the hotel to board either one.

Corporal Koonce rode up to the warehouse shortly after Larabee got back to tell him what he had already suspected, that the train today would have a big shipment of goods destined for Fort Wallace.

"We'll have some soldiers here to help you and Julio Romeriz load it on the wagons," Koonce said.

"You'll head out for Wallace first thing in the morning just like before. Say, I had a hot time last night. Went to one of the fancy saloons for a change, the Golden Eagle."

"Any different from the others?" Larabee asked with little interest. To his way of thinking, Koonce talked too much.

"Girl I met there sure was. She wasn't one of the girls who worked there. She just dropped in to look for some excitement. Black hair, brown eyes, and a happy-go-lucky way of doing things."

Larabee's interest quickened. "Did she tell you her name?"

"Sure," Koonce said. "Brenda Bailey. Just came in from Kansas City. Said the town was pretty dull and she was looking for excitement."

Larabee stared down the street toward the hotel. He and Brenda hadn't seen eye to eye on everything, but he hadn't thought their disagreement had reached the point where she'd go out deliberately looking for excitement.

"I knew her," he said finally. "She came here to meet a man. If I were you, I'd go a little easy."

Koonce laughed. "As long as she's willing, I'm not going to hold back. If this other fellow wants to keep his property, he'd better show up."

"He just might do that," Larabee said.

Tully O'Brien came in then. "I've got a big shipment coming in on today's train," he said. "Could you help me shift things around so I'll have room for it?"

"Sure," Larabee said. "I won't have anything to do until the train gets here."

Koonce went outside and mounted his horse. Larabee wasn't surprised when he rode up the street toward the saloons and hotel instead of back to the army camp.

"What needs to be moved?" Larabee asked, deliberately pushing Brenda and Koonce out of his mind.

"I have to move these whiskey barrels over against that wall," Tully said. "They're full, so it will be a big job."

Misti came into the warehouse, followed by Annie with her arm in a sling.

"Going out snake-hunting today?" Larabee asked with a grin.

Annie shuddered. "I don't want to ever see another rattler."

Misti looked at Larabee. "I don't see how you can even joke about it."

"Might as well joke about it as cry," Larabee said.

"You'll eat dinner with us, won't you?" Misti asked Larabee. "I want to know how many places to set."

"Looks like I'd better pay board and room here," Larabee said.

"You're more than earning your keep," Tully said. Then he turned to Misti. "Of course he'll eat with us. You didn't need to ask."

"Pa!" Annie broke in. "She wanted to ask."

"Annie!" Misti exclaimed, her face flushing.

Larabee felt his own face burning a little, and he was disgusted with himself. But it suddenly struck him that if Koonce had been making remarks about Misti like he had about Brenda, the corporal might have ended up with a bloody nose. It made Larabee think a little.

"I'll be here for dinner," Larabee said, then turned to help Tully move the barrels.

The barrels were not hard to move when the two men worked together. But when Larabee gave one barrel a jerk to tip it up on its rim, the barrel almost came over on top of him.

"Hey, this barrel is empty," he exclaimed. "Somebody gypped you."

"They did for a fact," Tully said, anger flushing his face as he tipped the barrel with one hand. "Don't feel like there was a drop in it."

Larabee turned the barrel over. The bung was out of it, and it showed marks of having had a spigot screwed into the hole.

"They must have emptied that before they shipped it," Larabee said.

"I suppose so, but it seems odd we didn't discover it when we unloaded the barrels from the train."

A little farther on, they found another empty barrel with the same markings on it. Then the very next barrel Larabee grabbed hold of refused to budge at all. He gave it a second jerk as Tully caught hold of the other side and heaved. Still the barrel refused to move.

"Something's holding it down," Tully said.

Suddenly Larabee saw the whole picture. "Hold on a minute," he said, and went outside. Jumping off the platform, he stooped over and made his way under the floor of the warehouse. About where he thought the barrel should be, he saw what he was looking for.

A spigot was pointed downward from a hole in the floor of the warehouse. Larabee turned the spigot a trifle, and whiskey poured out on the ground. Now he understood that hissing sound he had heard some nights when he was trying to sleep up in the warehouse. Zeke Quincey had been draining whiskey from the barrels.

Larabee went back upstairs and told Tully what he had found and what he was sure had been happening.

"Here I thought he was just a harmless drunk who liked to hang around the warehouse when he got in off work," Tully said angrily. "Never thought he was stealing me blind. I've seen him leaning against these barrels. He must have been sliding them around so that the bung was right over those holes in the floor. He's pretty clever to get that bung out and the spigot in without spilling a lot of whiskey."

"From the smell of things down there, I'd say he did spill a lot," Larabee said. "But he also saved a lot for drinking."

"He couldn't drink three barrels of it," Tully said incredulously. "Just wait till he gets here tonight! He's got some explaining to do."

"I just thought he was trying to save a hotel bill," Larabee said.

"He'll find this is a lot more expensive than a hotel when he gets through paying for those three barrels of whiskey," Tully said angrily. "Let's get the rest of these barrels moved."

They found no more empty barrels, and they soon had a space cleared for the freight due in on the train. By the time they had finished, Misti called them to dinner.

After he ate, Larabee managed to find things to do around the warehouse until the train whistled east of town. He went outside then to be ready to unload the army supplies. He saw Corporal Koonce coming from the hotel, and he guessed he had been there to see Brenda. At least Brenda would have something to do while Larabee was at Fort Wallace, unless the lieutenant assigned Koonce to the escort detail again.

Larabee suddenly remembered the telegram he had received. Clyde Voss might be on this train today. If so, Larabee had better meet him. Certainly he didn't want the lawyer to land in Sheridan and not be able to find him because he had gone to Fort Wallace. Larabee couldn't imagine what Tom Gleye wanted to tell him that was so important he'd send a man all the way out here from Kansas City instead of writing Larabee a letter.

If the lawyer was on the train, Larabee would have to arrange a meeting with him later today, for he had work to do now. But occupying more of his thoughts than the lawyer were the men who had robbed him. He was sure they were still in town. Only a drummer and two businessmen from Kansas City had gone out on the stage to Denver this morning.

Tully O'Brien was getting very impatient. If Larabee didn't put his finger on those men soon, the vigilantes would begin acting. And with no more evidence than they had, they could easily hang the wrong men.

CHAPTER 11

The train slowed as it came in sight, finally halting at the depot. Larabee stood on the platform and watched the passengers come down the steps that the conductor let down.

He was surprised at the number of people getting off the train. There were three women, latecomers to the thriving business fostered by the saloons. Seven men got off the train. Larabee studied them all, but he had no idea what Voss looked like, and there wasn't a man among the seven that looked to him like a lawyer.

Down the platform a short distance Slip Neff had stopped one of the men who had gotten off the train and was talking to him. He was a small man wearing spectacles. He didn't look like a gambler, but Larabee supposed he must be one since Neff seemed to know him intimately.

After they had talked a while, they moved off toward the hotel on the north side of the tracks from the depot. They made an odd-looking pair going into the hotel. Neff was a small man, standing only five and a half feet tall. But the bespectacled man who had come in on the train was even smaller.

Two army wagons rolled up to one of the cars farther back in the train. Julio Romeriz was driving one of them, and a soldier was handling the reins on the other. Larabee turned that way. The army wouldn't like it if he didn't get to work on the job he had been hired to do.

When the two wagons were loaded, they were as full as they had been on the previous trip. The sun was getting over toward the west when Larabee drove his team up the tracks and turned north past the livery barn to the soldiers' camp on the plateau above the ravine. He was impatient to get back to the warehouse to be with Tully when they faced Zeke Quincey. Larabee couldn't imagine what Quincey had done with all that whiskey.

"It's up to you two to watch these wagons tonight," one of the soldiers said when they reached the edge of the camp.

"We'll watch them," Romeriz said. "But nobody's going to run off with these wagons this close to the camp."

The soldiers rode on toward the sod-and-pole shelter they had erected for their horses. The soldiers' quarters were frame, one of the few frame buildings anywhere in Sheridan. It pointed up one of the paradoxes of this town. The businessmen, many of them conducting their businesses in tents, talked of future plans for the city, although they all agreed that Sheridan would lose much of its population when the construction crews moved on. The soldiers' camp was here just until the rails reached Fort Wallace. No one even hinted that the camp might remain, yet it had much more permanent quarters than did most of the inhabitants of the town.

"Are you going to stay with the wagons?" Larabee asked Romeriz.

The Mexican nodded. "I'll bunk here like I always do. Have you got some business in town again?"

"Some," Larabee said. "I'll be back as soon as it's finished."

"Throw your blankets under your wagon," Romeriz said. "Don't wake me up when you get in. I want a good night's sleep."

As soon as the teams were taken care of, Larabee headed for town. It was only a short distance to O'Brien's Warehouse where he wanted to be when the work train pulled in tonight.

Misti was at the warehouse when Larabee walked in. He could see from Frank Woods' face that they had been having an argument. He wondered why Misti was here if she didn't want to see Woods.

"Will you be going to Fort Wallace tomorrow?" she asked Larabee.

He nodded. "We're all loaded and ready to pull out at dawn."

"Do you expect any Indian trouble like you had last time?"

"We always try to be ready for that," Larabee said. "I think the lieutenant will send an escort with us again. You're not worried about it, are you?"

Misti glanced at him, then at Woods, then back to him. "Indians always worry me," she said. "Will you come over for supper?"

He grinned. "Getting so I feel like I belong there," he said.

"You're acting like you owned the whole family," Woods said curtly, and went back into his little office.

Larabee stared after him. "He must have a burr under his saddle. Listen. Here comes the work train."

Misti looked out the back door toward the house. "Here comes Pa, too. He's been waiting for that train. I'll see you at supper."

She went out the back door and down the steps,

meeting Tully just as he was about to ascend. Larabee waited until Tully came in.

"Going to meet the train or wait here for him to show up?"

"I'll wait, " Tully said. "He always comes here, and now I know why."

Woods poked his head out of the office. "Who are you expecting?" he asked.

"Quincey," Tully said. "I've got a question to ask him."

Woods appeared on the verge of saying something else, then pinched his lips together and turned back to his work.

The train stopped, and the few men who came back to town with it each night got off. Zeke Quincey was one of those who swung down, and he headed straight for O'Brien's Warehouse. Since the work train usually made its first stop close to the water tank, O'Brien's was about the nearest business place.

Quincey sat down on the steps of the warehouse as he always did. Larabee had thought little of that before, but now he saw that Quincey was likely sizing up the situation from there. He could see underneath the floor to the area where he got his whiskey. He wasn't going to go back there, however, until he was sure he could do it unobserved. From the steps he could see into the warehouse and also look over town and make sure no one passing along the street would see him disappear under the warehouse.

Tully stepped to the door. "Quincey, come in here," he said.

The construction worker looked up in surprise. Tully usually ignored him, and there was an urgency in Tully's voice now that was bound to stir alarm in Quincey.

"Got some errand for me to do?" Quincey said, coming up the steps into the warehouse.

"Got some questions to ask you," Tully said.

Woods had come out of the office and was standing close by, listening attentively. Larabee moved up beside Tully. Quincey was going to think that Larabee had gone back on his word not to tell Tully that he was staying under the warehouse. But when Larabee had promised that, he had assumed that all Quincey was doing under there was sleeping, thus saving the price of a room at the hotel. Now that stealing was involved, it put things in a different light. If Quincey couldn't see that, Larabee wasn't going to worry about it.

"I've got two empty whiskey barrels and another one fastened to the floor with a spigot screwed into the bung," Tully said. "What do you know about it?"

"Why should I know anything about it?" Quincey said, looking accusingly at Larabee.

"You sleep under there every night," Tully said. "You've been stealing that whiskey. You might as well admit it."

Quincey shook his head. "I ain't admitting nothing like that. I need a drink now."

"You're not going to get one until you tell me what you've been doing with that whiskey you've been stealing."

Larabee saw Woods duck back into the office and come out with his hat. It was almost closing time, so he supposed Woods had decided he might as well go on home. This discussion didn't concern him.

"I need a drink before I tell you anything," Quincey repeated.

Larabee saw the anger rising in Tully's face. In

spite of knowing now that Quincey was a thief, Larabee had come to like the ruddy-faced worker. He supposed that was partly because he had helped him trace down the shirt with the missing button.

"I know you've been taking that whiskey," Tully said almost gently. "Nobody's going to hang you for that. But I want to know some other things. You might as well tell me."

Quincey looked around as if searching for a place to hide. Then he took a deep breath and faced Tully.

"All right. So I stole some of your whiskey. A man like me don't earn enough to buy all the whiskey he wants."

"You couldn't drink three barrels of it," Tully said. "Did you waste most of it getting the spigot screwed in?"

Quincey shook his head. "Naw. I didn't waste much. I put a big bucket under the barrel before I knocked out the bung. Didn't have too much trouble screwing in the spigot, either. It's not as hard to do as you might think."

"Did you bore a hole in the platform to come up right under the bung on a barrel?" Larabee asked.

Quincey grinned as he warmed to his description of how he had maneuvered the theft. "Most of these planks in the floor were rafted down the river before they were shipped out here by train, you know," he said. "Somebody bored big holes in the ends of the boards so they could tie the raft together with ropes. I found one of the barrels with the bung hole right over one of these holes. That's where I got the idea. After that barrel was empty, I managed to shift other barrels over other holes when I came down here before closing time. Sometimes I had to shift a barrel a couple of times before I got it where I could knock out the bung and screw in the spigot."

Tully stared at Quincey in amazement. "I'll be a cross-eyed leprechaun!" he muttered. "You were stealing me blind right while I was watching you."

"You couldn't have drunk all that whiskey yourself," Larabee said.

"I can drink more than you think I can," Quincey said proudly.

"Not three barrels of it," Tully said. "What did you do with the rest?"

Quincey squirmed uncomfortably. "I sold it," he said finally.

"Sold it!" Tully exclaimed. "I thought you were just a worthless drunk and a petty thief. How much did you sell?"

"Enough to pay a man to keep quiet about me stealing what I wanted to drink."

Tully looked at Larabee. "He can't mean you?"

Larabee shook his head. "He didn't pay me anything. I knew he was there, but I didn't know he was stealing the whiskey."

"It wasn't him," Quincey said. "I was caught stealing a little whiskey to drink. Guess I was pretty drunk and got careless. Anyway, this fellow said he'd keep quiet about what I was doing if I'd pay him five dollars a day. I have to sell a lot of whiskey to raise that much every day."

Larabee recalled the man in the hotel hallway. "You were selling it in the hotel, weren't you?"

Quincey nodded. "I had to sell it quite a bit cheaper than they sell it at the saloons, of course, but I've got some regular customers now."

"Who was blackmailing you?" Tully demanded.

"He'll kill me if I tell," Quincey whimpered. "I need a drink."

"I'll kill you if you don't," Tully said in a tone that left no doubt that the immediate danger was much more potent than any delayed threat.

"It was Frank Woods," Quincey said in a whisper. "He worked late one night and heard me under the warehouse. He came down and caught me."

"Woods!" Tully exclaimed. "I didn't think he'd do a thing like that."

"He didn't steal the whiskey," Quincey said. "He made me do that."

"He was taking stolen money," Tully said. "He might just as well have stolen the whiskey. Maybe he did steal some, too, when you were gone and nobody was looking."

"Why didn't you let Woods talk?" Larabee asked. "That would have been better than what you did."

"I reckon it would have," Quincey admitted. "But I figured if anybody else found out what I was doing, I'd lose my job on the railroad. And even worse, the vigilantes might hang me."

"That's an idea," Tully said. "But I don't think the vigilantes will waste a rope on a whiskey thief. Where did Frank go?"

Larabee went to the street door and looked down toward the hotel. "I saw him leave," he said. "I figured he was just going home."

"He probably guessed we were going to find out about him," Tully said angrily. "Taking a bribe from a man stealing my whiskey was bad, but he was two-faced enough to go on working for me and drawing my wages while he was doing it. I'll have his hide for that."

Misti came to the back door then to say that supper was ready. Tully closed the front door of the warehouse. When he came to the back door, Quincey was still there.

"What are you going to do with me?" Quincy asked.

"I haven't figured that out yet," Tully said. "You've cost me almost three barrels of whiskey."

"I'll pay you back," Quincey said eagerly, "if you just don't turn me over to the vigilantes or tell my boss what I've done."

"You can't very well pay me back if you lose your job," Tully said. "You go on to wherever you're going to spend the night. I won't tell your boss. But don't let me catch you under my warehouse again."

"You won't!" Quincey promised, and went down the steps in two giant strides, then headed up the street toward the saloons and the hotel.

Before supper was quite over, a man rapped sharply on the door, and Tully opened it.

"What's wrong, Bert?" he asked.

"Frank Woods held up the general store and knifed the clerk when he refused to hand over all the money. Thought you ought to know since he works for you."

"He doesn't work for me any more," Tully said sharply.

He closed the door and turned back to the others in the room. "What do you make of that, Dave?"

"He must be planning to skip out," Larabee said. "He evidently thought you'd be pretty hard on him when you found out what he'd been up to. And he knew you were going to find out."

"So he robbed the store to get a little extra money before he left."

"Does he own a horse?" Larabee asked.

Tully nodded. "Keeps him at the livery stable across from the water tank."

"He has probably already left town," Larabee said. "But I'll run down to the barn just in case he hasn't pulled out yet."

Larabee hurried outside and ran down the street toward the livery barn. He was crossing the tracks close to the water tank when he saw a rider come out of the barn and ride south past the east side of the twin buttes, kicking his horse to its fastest pace.

Running hard, Larabee burst into the barn. "Who was that riding out?" he demanded.

"Frank Woods," the liveryman said. "He was acting queer. Came down here half an hour ago and saddled his horse, then left him here and went up the street. Now he comes back and rides out like Satan was on his tail."

"Say where he was going?"

"He didn't say a word. Just grabbed his horse and lit out."

Larabee spotted a horse in a stall with the saddle still on. "I'll take that horse for a few minutes."

"He hasn't been grained," the liveryman objected. "Bill Pollack had him out for a short ride somewhere."

Larabee tightened the cinch and wheeled the horse out of the barn.

The horse was a long-legged bay, and Larabee guessed he was fast. Woods had a good head start, but there was still an hour of daylight left. Larabee hoped he could overtake the clerk before darkness set in.

He spurred the horse past the twin buttes, then checked the horizon in every direction. Off to the southeast, Larabee saw a rider. Woods apparently was trying to circle the town and go east. There was nowhere west for a man with Woods' capabilities to survive. He had to head back toward civilization.

Larabee discovered that he had not misjudged the horse under him. He was even faster than he had anticipated. In twenty minutes, he had gained enough ground that he was no longer afraid that he would not be able to overtake Woods before dark. Still his horse was running easily, and the horse Woods was riding appeared to be about all in. Woods probably hadn't ridden him enough to have him toughened up, Larabee guessed, and he was the kind who wouldn't let anyone else ride his horse.

The sun was just setting when Larabee came within hailing distance of Woods. Larabee had his gun strapped around his waist, but he didn't want to have to use it. He didn't know whether Woods had a gun or not. He had used a knife on that clerk.

Woods ignored Larabee's yell, so when Larabee got closer he fired a shot over Woods' head. The clerk suddenly yanked back on his reins and stopped, his hands held high.

Larabee rode up cautiously but Woods was thoroughly cowed. Larabee took the knife he had in the sheath under his left arm and pointed Woods' weary horse back toward Sheridan.

It was after dark when they got back to the livery barn. Larabee turned the horses over to the stableman without any explanation and guided Woods up the street past the water tank to O'Brien's place.

Larabee found a light in the warehouse and the back door open. Instead of taking Woods to the house, he guided him up the steps into the warehouse. Tully was there along with Ray Horton, the barber, and they had Zeke Quincey with them.

"Where can you lock him up?" Larabee asked. "You don't have a jail, do you?"

"We don't need a jail," Tully said. "He won't have to wait long for a trial."

"The vigilantes don't give a man a fair trial," Woods whimpered.

"You ought to know," Larabee said. "You were one of them."

"Every man gets a fair trial from the vigilantes," Tully said sharply.

Larabee nodded at Quincey. "What are you going to do with him?"

"We brought him here to testify at Frank's trial. We figured you'd bring him back."

"I don't want to testify," Quincey whimpered.

"We're not asking you what you want to do," Tully said sharply. "You'll tell the truth if we have to whip it out of you. You'll be needed, too, Dave."

"When will it be?" Larabee asked, thinking of his trip tomorrow to Fort Wallace.

"About an hour from now," Tully said.

"I'll be here," Larabee said.

"I need a drink," Quincey begged.

"You'll get along without one for a while," Tully said. "Dave, I'm leaving you in charge of these two. Ray and I have some men to see. The trial will be held right here in an hour."

Larabee watched Tully O'Brien and Ray Horton go out the door. Looking at the two men he was guarding, he couldn't help thinking how he'd feel if he were in their place. Going on trial before the vigilantes, whose dreaded sentence was the rope, was something he hever wanted to experience.

CHAPTER 12

Promptly at the hour Tully had set, three hooded men appeared in the rear doorway of the warehouse, quickly came inside, then stepped back where they couldn't be seen by anyone passing along behind the warehouse. A minute later two more came. Others came at short intervals until nearly twenty men, all wearing hoods over their heads that reached down past their shoulders, were assembled.

"Judge, take over," one man grunted, his words muffled through the cloth of his hood.

Larabee tried to identify some of the men but realized he could only guess who anyone was although he was sure he'd recognize several of them without their hoods. He wondered if they wore the hoods at every meeting. Perhaps they were being extra careful this time because they didn't want him or Zeke Quincey to be able to identify them later. It didn't make any difference about Woods. He already knew who they were.

A big man stepped up beside Larabee. "Frank Woods," he said in a low monotone, "you are charged with blackmail and assault with a knife during the act of robbery. How do you plead to those charges?"

"It ain't as bad as it sounds," Woods whimpered. "I had to have money, and that simple-minded clerk wouldn't give it to me."

"Everybody has to have money," the man droned. "How do you plead?"

"He wouldn't have gotten hurt if he'd done what he was told," Woods said in a louder voice.

The man doing the questioning turned to the others. "He pleads guilty to assault with a knife during a robbery." He turned back to the prisoner. "What about the charge of blackmail in connection with the whiskey stolen from the O'Brien Warehouse?"

Woods pointed a shaking finger at Zeke Quincey. "There's the thief. He's the one who should be on trial."

"We'll get to him later," the judge said. "You're on trial now."

"I didn't steal that whiskey," Woods almost shouted. "Quincey paid me not to tell Tully he was stealing it. I needed the money, so I took it."

"Why did you need so much money? You had a good job."

"A man with plans to get married needs a lot of money," Woods said. "My salary wasn't enough to keep two people."

"Just who did you figure on sharing this wealth with?" the judge asked.

Woods bristled. "What business is that of yours?" Then he wilted like an uprooted sunflower in a hot sun. "Misti O'Brien," he said in a whisper.

The hooded man who had opened the meeting suddenly leaped forward and hit Woods, sending him reeling back against the whiskey barrels. The judge caught the man's arm as he started to follow Woods.

"This is his trial, not his execution," the judge snapped.

The man stepped back into the ranks of hooded

men, still without saying a word. Larabee no longer had to guess which man was Tully O'Brien.

"Dave Larabee, step up here," the judge called.

Two hooded men moved over to stand on either side of Frank Woods while Larabee stepped up to face the judge. Larabee was asked to tell what he knew about the disappearance of the whiskey. Quickly he told his story, then Zeke Quincey was called up.

Quincey admitted taking the whiskey. "But I would never have taken any more than I could drink myself," he said, his voice cracking with fear as he faced the hooded jury, "if Woods hadn't caught me and threatened to turn me over to the vigilantes unless I paid them to keep quiet. The only way I could get that money was to steal more whiskey and sell it to people I knew over at the hotel."

Quincey was released, and one of the hooded men whose name was not used told how he had stepped into the store just in time to see Woods stab the clerk and grab the money, then dash out the back door.

The judge turned to the men. "Anybody know how Carl is doing?"

"He wasn't hurt bad," one man said. "Doc says he'll be all right in a few days."

Woods was called back then. "Do you have anything to say before we vote?" the judge asked.

"I've been a good clerk for Tully," Woods whimpered. "Just ask him."

"Nobody here answers to the name of Tully," the judge said distinctly. "Anyway, you're not being judged on how good a clerk you were. Let's take the vote."

The two men held on to Woods' arms. Larabee had seen the clerk's desperate glance around as if weighing his chances of escape. A man stepped out of the ranks and handed a slip of paper to each man.

"You know the three possibilities," the judge said. "Cast your vote."

A pencil was passed around among the men; then the slips were collected and handed to the judge. He unfolded the papers and read them aloud while a man kept a tally.

Larabee watched in amazement. It was like an election for president of a school literary. But a man's life was hanging in the balance here. The judge had mentioned three alternatives, but there were only two given among the slips turned in. Larabee guessed the other alternative would have been not guilty.

Only three of the twenty votes were to hang the prisoner. The judge looked up after the last vote was counted.

"Frank Woods, you have until daylight to get out of Sheridan and never return. If you do, you will hang."

Relief swept over Woods' face. "I'll be gone," he promised.

"You will take nothing with you but your horse and three days' rations," the judge went on. "Any other possessions you may have accumulated will go to pay Carl's doctor bill."

Woods nodded vigorously to show his acceptance of the verdict, then almost ran out the door when the hooded guards released him. The judge turned then to Quincey and motioned him forward. He stepped up, his trembling knees threatening to give way with him.

"I ain't got no other place to go," he whimpered.

Obviously Quincey no longer feared the rope from this jury because his crime would hardly equal that of Woods, but he was expecting to be run out of town, and that would mean losing his job, which he probably hoped to keep until the tracks reached Denver.

"He ought to have to pay Tully for the whiskey he stole," one man said. "Half his wages until his debt is paid."

The judge looked over the men. "How does that sound?"

Heads nodded in agreement, and the judge passed the sentence. Quincey accepted it eagerly and even promised more than half his wages to settle the debt.

One man stepped outside the back door and looked around, then turned back, motioning to the others. By twos and threes, they went outside and down the steps. Larabee guessed that the men would take off their hoods and put them into their pockets before stepping out on the street. Only a close observer would guess that they were coming from a vigilante meeting.

When the last of the vigilantes were gone, Larabee and Quincey went out the door. Larabee saw Tully standing by the door of his house and went over.

"Why are the vigilantes so careful not to let anyone see their faces?" he asked. "There's no law here to arrest them for doing what they're doing."

"The outlaw element would have some hangings of its own if any of the vigilantes could be positively identified," Tully said. "Will you be staying in the warehouse tonight, Dave?"

"I have to stay with my wagon at the soldier camp," Larabee said.

Tully went on to shut up the warehouse while Larabee moved around the building to the street. Quincey was right behind him.

"I learned something today after work that might be worth a dollar to you," he said.

Thinking of the shirt Quincey had found, Larabee nodded, fishing a dollar out of his pocket. "What?"

"I overheard you say you were looking for a lawyer from Kansas City. He's in town."

"How do you know?"

"I heard some fellows in the Cross-Tie talking about him. He's a little fellow with thick glasses."

"I saw that man talking to Slip Neff," Larabee exclaimed. "But he didn't look like a lawyer to me." He realized he should have suspected every man who got off the train of being the lawyer. "Do you know where he is now?"

"All I heard was that the lawyer was in town."

"Who said so?"

"I didn't know the fellows who were talking," Quincey said. "One was a little man, looked like a gambler, and the other one was about your size."

"Could have been Neff and Steve Gleye," Larabee said thoughtfully. "Thanks, Zeke."

Quincey headed up the near side of the tracks, but Larabee crossed over to the north side and started toward the main part of town. It was late, but there were lights in most of the saloons.

The Golden Eagle Saloon was still crowded, and Larabee had to push his way through to the table where Neff was sitting with four other men. The hand was just finishing, and Neff was raking in the pot. Before the cards could be dealt again, Larabee laid a hand on the gambler's shoulder.

Neff looked up, then frowned. "What do you want?"

"A few words with you," Larabee said.

"Can't you see I don't have time for idle gossip? I'm busy."

Larabee's fingers bit into Neff's shoulder. "You're going to be busier in a minute if you don't talk to me."

Angrily, Neff pushed back his chair. He shoved the cards toward the player next to him. "You shuffle. Deal me in. I'll be back in time to play my hand."

Neff hurried toward a corner where there were no people at the moment. "Now speak your piece, and make it fast."

"I will," Larabee said. "Where is Clyde Voss?"

"Who is Clyde Voss?" Neff demanded, and Larabee guessed that the gambler had anticipated the question and was braced for it.

"The lawyer you met at the train this afternoon. I want to talk to him."

"I don't know any Voss?" Neff said.

"I don't care what name you call him by," Larabee said, his anger rising. "I want to know where the little man is that you met at the train."

"Who said I met the train?" Neff demanded.

"I do," Larabee said. "I saw you. And I saw you take that little man with the thick glasses toward the hotel. Now I want to know what you did with him."

Larabee gripped Neff again by the shoulder, but suddenly Neff whipped around and brought up a knife. "Don't try to run over me," the little gambler hissed.

Larabee stepped back quickly, his hand on his gun

butt. "You try carving me up, Neff, and you'll get a bullet in the brisket."

Neff glared at Larabee for a moment, then slowly put the knife away. "I took the man to see Steve," he said finally. "After all, he is Tom Gleye's lawyer."

"Why didn't you tell me that in the first place?" Larabee grunted. "It would have saved you some trouble."

Larabee wheeled toward the door and pushed his way out into the street. Turning down the street, he passed the Cross-Tie and stepped up on the porch of the hotel. The clerk had gone to bed, but there was a man in the lobby, dozing.

"Have you seen a small man with heavy glasses?" Larabee asked.

The man opened his eyes and stared sleepily at Larabee. "I haven't seen anybody," he said. "Not even the clerk so I can get a room. I'm going to spend a free night right here."

Larabee turned to the stairs. He remembered seeing Steve Gleye's name listed under Room 28 when he'd looked at the register last night. Steve wouldn't have the lawyer in his own room unless he wanted to keep Larabee from seeing him, but Larabee was convinced now that was what was afoot. It began to look like Neff was working with Steve, too. That didn't make much sense because Steve owed Neff a small fortune.

Room 28 was locked, and there was no light inside. Larabee knocked and listened carefully. If anyone was inside, he was sure he could hear him breathe even if he didn't move. The walls and doors were thin enough to let any sound come through. But there was no sound.

After looking through the hotel and the Cross-Tie Saloon where he expected to find Steve and didn't, Larabee headed back for the soldier camp. He hated to give up the search, but he had no idea where else to look, and he needed some rest before the trip tomorrow.

It was late when he reached the wagons. The lights were out in the soldiers' quarters, and Larabee rolled up in his blankets under his wagon and tried to get to sleep. Tomorrow could be another tension-filled day. Any trip from Sheridan to Fort Wallace these days, with the Indians on the prod, could be quite an experience.

Reveille at the soldier barracks brought Larabee awake. He crawled out of his blankets and rolled them ready to toss on the wagon. Glancing over, he saw that Romeriz hadn't stirred yet. That was odd, for the Mexican had been up and stirring before reveille sounded the morning they had been at Fort Wallace.

Larabee started toward the barn to feed the mules, thinking he'd go to mess with the soldiers. As he passed Romeriz's wagon, he saw that the freighter still hadn't moved.

Then he saw blood on the blankets and noticed that they were rumpled and twisted. Hurrying over, he dropped to one knee beside the Mexican freighter. Before he touched him, he knew he was dead. Someone had stabbed him several times while he was asleep.

Larabee's first impulse was to dash to the barracks and alert the soldiers. Then he realized that if there were any clues, a dozen soldiers running around would soon wipe them out.

Carefully, Larabee searched the area. There were footprints, but, this close to the barracks and the barns, that meant nothing. The knife that had been used was not here. This had not been a careless, sloppy job. Apparently it had been well planned and executed. So far as Larabee knew, Julio Romeriz had no enemies anywhere in Sheridan.

Larabee's next conclusion was one that shook him a little. There had been two or three tries made on his life. Whoever had murdered Julio Romeriz might have thought he was plunging that knife into Larabee.

Another idea pestered Larabee. Could Steve Gleye have had a hand in this? Larabee didn't think Steve was capable of killing a man with a knife, but he could have planned it. Maybe that was where Steve had been the previous night when Larabee was looking for him at the hotel and the Cross-Tie. He had never before thought of Steve as a mortal enemy, but somebody here in Sheridan was.

Larabee reported what had happened to Corporal Koonce at the barracks, and the soldiers swarmed over the area almost immediately. Larabee, thinking of Steve, headed for town without waiting for breakfast. He didn't have anything but a hunch on which to base his suspicions, but, in thinking back, there hadn't been a time when his life had been in danger that Steve couldn't have been the man behind it. He resolved to find out if his hunch had any solid foundation.

The town was just starting to stir when Larabee walked up the street. Steve would likely be at the hotel asleep. At the hotel, Larabee went up the steps of the porch in one leap. The clerk wasn't at the desk yet, and the whole building seemed to be quiet. It wouldn't be for long, Larabee resolved. Going up the stairs, he stopped in front of Room 28. He hammered on the door and waited.

When there was no sound inside, he hammered again. The door of a room down the hall opened. Larabee turned to see Slip Neff peering out sleepily.

"Can't you let anybody sleep?" Neff demanded.

"Where's Steve?" Larabee asked.

"He found another place to stay," Neff said. "He didn't like this hotel."

Larabee turned back to the door he'd been pounding on. Turning the knob, he found that the door was unlocked. Pushing it open, he saw that the bed was empty. Wheeling back to Neff, Larabee crossed to the door.

"Where was Steve last night?"

"How do I know?" Neff replied irritably. "I was playing cards. I'm going to be playing again tonight, so I need some sleep now. Get out of the hotel before you wake up everybody."

Larabee turned away, frustration sweeping over him. There were a dozen places where Steve could be staying, but Larabee didn't have time to search him out.

CHAPTER 13

Slip Neff stood in his doorway and watched Larabee turn and go down the stairs. That had been close. He was glad he'd made Steve change rooms again, even if the clerk had thought he was crazy.

As soon as Larabee was out of the building, Neff went to his window and looked down the street. Larabee was going back toward the soldier camp. It had been a shock seeing Larabee this morning. But he had wondered last night when Steve reported that Cottier had done his job if things had worked out the way they had planned. Steve's report had come too soon after Neff had been arguing with Larabee.

It was early, but Neff felt an urgency that didn't submit to time. Going down the hall to Room 22, he rapped sharply on the door. Inside there was a grunt, and after the second rap, Steve opened the door.

"What's the idea of getting a man up in the middle of the night?" Steve demanded grumpily.

"I've already had company," Neff said, pushing the door open and crowding in past Steve. "Larabee was up here looking for you."

Steve's eyes widened, and he came awake. "Larabee? Cottier told me he killed him last night down at the soldiers' camp."

"He lied to you," Neff said. "Maybe he killed somebody else like he did out on the Smoky Hill."

"What did Larabee want?" Steve asked after a moment.

"You," Neff said. "He didn't say what for. But I have a hunch he's still looking for that lawyer." Neff shook his head in disgust. "And you didn't want to move your room."

"Pete said he had killed Larabee," Steve said defensively. "Why should I make another move just to dodge a corpse? I'm glad we didn't pay off Pete."

"Cottier is an ignorant blockhead," Neff said. "We can't trust him to do anything right. Larabee is still alive and very suspicious. We've got to do something quick. And we're going to have to do it ourselves. How is the lawyer making out?"

Steve's eyes shot to a corner of the dresser where a key lay. "He hasn't given any trouble. That room he is in can't be opened without a key, and I'm keeping that. Anyway, he's so scared, he won't try to get away. I told him that if he tried to escape, I'd hang him from a rafter with just his toes touching the floor and leave him there till he died. He believed me."

"Have you checked this morning to make sure he didn't get away?" Neff asked.

"Of course not," Steve said irritably. "You woke me up."

"I'll feel safer when I know he's still in his room."

Steve tossed the key to Neff. "Check for yourself."

Neff took the key and stepped out into the hall. The night before, they had rented the room that had the best lock in the hotel and put Voss in it. Later Neff had made Steve switch his room to the one next to Voss so he could hear any movement Voss made and also to keep Larabee from finding Steve, just in case Cottier hadn't done his job. Neff had been sure that Larabee knew by now that Steve was supposed to be in Room 28.

Steve was right about not being able to trust Cottier to do a job. But Neff would carry this lack of dependability one step further. Neff couldn't trust Steve to do things right, either. Neff stood to gain too much from this factory in Toledo to let it slip away because of his partners' bungling. But he couldn't just eliminate both partners and take it all for himself as he had done in some of his other deals. Steve held the key to everything here. Without him, there would be no inheritance for Neff to grab.

Neff put the key in the lock and turned it. He pushed open the door a crack and peeked in. Clyde Voss, the lawyer, was wide awake but still in bed, staring fearfully at the door. Neff closed the door and locked it again. At least Steve had been right about the lawyer's staying where he had been put. But it had been Neff's idea to confine him in this room and also to move Steve down here beside him. Left alone, Steve would have bungled it all.

Neff went back to Steve's room, thinking hard. There ought to be some way he could manage things so he'd get that Toledo factory without having to depend on Steve Gleye. If he could work out such a plan, he'd eliminate his partners and carry on himself. Then he'd be sure of success.

"He's there, all right," Neff said. "What do you intend to do with him?"

"Send him back where he came from," Steve said. "He's scared enough now that he'll go back and keep his mouth shut."

Neff shook his head. "He may know too much."

"How could he? He hasn't talked to anybody but

us. I told him that Dave Larabee had left town and that a lawyer from the city would be almost sure to be killed if he stayed around here. I convinced him that I'm sending him back to Kansas City to save his life."

"You don't think a lawyer will swallow that, do you?" Neff asked.

"Voss will," Steve said confidently. "He's so scared now he can't spit. I figure he'll run for that train when it's ready to pull out."

"If he learns anything about our plans, we'll have to kill him," Neff said. "I'm going down to breakfast."

"I'm going to bring breakfast up to Voss," Steve said. "No sense in having him mixing with other people."

"I agree," Neff said, and went back up the hall to his room.

Neff had some planning to do. The way his partners had bungled things left no doubt in his mind that he was going to have to do everything himself if he expected to get that shoe factory in Toledo.

There were two stumbling blocks. He couldn't eliminate either one of them just yet because he needed Steve to inherit that factory and he needed Cottier, bungler that he was, until he could get rid of Dave Larabee. Neff didn't mind admitting to himself that he was afraid of Larabee. He could handle most men, but not Larabee, and he knew it. He'd have to keep Cottier around to get rid of him.

As for Steve, there had to be a way to get that factory without him. And suddenly Neff thought he saw it. It would mean getting Steve to sign another paper, but Neff could maneuver that, all right. Once he got that paper signed and Cottier had killed Larabee, he'd find some way to get rid of Cottier. In fact, that would be very simple with the vigilantes just waiting to hang people who killed men like Dave Larabee.

Neff went down to breakfast full of his new plan. He waited for Steve, and they went in together, talking easily. Neff even offered to take Voss's breakfast up to him. Steve seemed a little puzzled, but he agreed quickly enough.

After feeding Voss and taking the empty plate back to the kitchen, Neff suggested to Steve that they pass the time of day with a card game. They had nothing to worry about from Larabee now because he should be taking a load of freight to Fort Wallace and wouldn't be back until the next day.

"I want to see Pete and find out what happened last night," Steve said.

Neff nodded. "So do I. After that, we'll have ourselves a game."

Neff knew how much Steve liked to gamble even though he was a poor hand with cards. He was depending on that to make his scheme work. They went to the tent where Pete Cottier rented a cot for twenty-five cents a night. There were two dozen buffalo hunters and idle construction workers in the tent. Cottier was up, but he hadn't had breakfast yet. Steve motioned for him to come outside, and Neff stayed in the background.

"What's eating on you this time of morning?" Cottier grumbled as he followed Steve around behind the tent.

"Didn't you say you killed Dave Larabee last night?"

"I sure did," Cottier said proudly. "Sneaked up on

him while he was sleeping under his wagon. Used a knife. He never knew what hit him."

"Good reason," Neff put in. "He didn't get hit."

Cottier turned on Neff angrily. "You're a liar. I know what I did."

"You didn't kill Larabee," Steve snapped. "He was at the hotel this morning looking for me."

Cottier glared at Steve then Neff as he accepted the fact that he had missed Larabee again. "I killed somebody," he muttered.

"I don't doubt that," Neff said. "You'd better hope it wasn't somebody who has friends among the vigilantes. Come on, Steve. He's got something to chew on for breakfast now."

"I want to make sure Voss gets on that train," Steve said.

"We won't let him miss it," Neff said. "Let's have a drink."

Neff led the way across the tracks and down the street a couple of doors to the Golden Eagle. He wanted familiar surroundings for the job ahead. The saloon was virtually empty at this hour.

As for Clyde Voss, Neff had already decided it was best for all concerned that the lawyer never go back to Kansas City. Steve was sure he hadn't heard any of their plans. But Neff had learned not to take such chances. If Voss didn't get back to Kansas City, he couldn't tell anything that he might have overheard. One more lawyer, dead or alive, wasn't going to make much of a ripple here in Sheridan.

Neff was depending on the fact that Steve never passed up a free drink to get his plan underway. Steve was at times a heavy drinker, and Neff was going to make sure this was one of those occasions.

Steve appeared a little suspicious of Neff's generosity in setting up the free drinks, but he didn't voice any objections. He was probably afraid the drinks would be withdrawn, Neff guessed.

When Steve began to lose his reasoning power, Neff brought out the cards. The train whistled for departure while Neff was dealing the third hand. But Steve already was concentrating every ounce of his whiskey-fogged brainpower on his cards and didn't even notice the whistle, much less remember that he intended to get Voss on that train.

Neff had let Steve win the first hand, but the whiskey was working well now, and Neff proceeded to up the ante on each hand, then rake in the pot. Steve's cash quickly vanished, and Neff shoved a paper at him that simply had an IOU on it. Steve signed it, and Neff raised the bet with each deal. By the time the saloon became crowded in the afternoon, Neff expected to have this game concluded to his complete satisfaction.

When Steve had signed over twenty thousand dollars in IOUs, Neff halted the game. Steve was no longer able to play intelligently. In fact, Neff doubted if he had any idea what he was doing.

Neff escorted Steve back to his hotel room. After checking on Voss, who was cowering in his room, Neff went back to the Golden Eagle, ready for an afternoon and evening of cards. But no game could now come close to being as profitable to him as the one he had just finished.

A dozen men were there who hadn't been when he left. Their talk was centered on the fatal stabbing of the Mexican freighter, Julio Romeriz, out by the soldier camp. Neff listened and said nothing. He soon learned that a soldier had driven Romeriz's wagon to Fort Wallace.

Steve didn't come to himself until the next morning. Neff had given Voss his breakfast. Now he took Steve aside and showed him the IOUs. As he expected, Steve denied ever having even seen them.

"What are you trying to pull?" he demanded angrily.

"Nothing," Neff said mildly. "I bought you some drinks, trying to be friendly, then we began a game. You insisted on upping the ante. When you ran out of money, you asked me to take your IOUs and I did."

"I was drunk," Steve snorted. "You knew that."

"I'm not your nursemaid," Neff said. "If you want to drink, that's your business. But when you owe me a debt, that's my business."

"I didn't know what I was doing—if I really did sign those," Steve said suspiciously. He glared at the papers. "You know I can't pay off."

"You're good for them," Neff said smugly. "You'll soon have plenty coming in from that Toledo factory."

"You're getting your third of that and that's all."

Neff shrugged. "I'm not asking for the factory, just some of the profits until your debt is paid. That should be fair enough."

Steve scowled. "Maybe so, if I intended to pay that debt. But I don't."

"It's an honest debt," Neff said sharply. "You'll pay it. Now I've already had the papers drawn up." He took a paper from his coat pocket. "This gives me thirty percent of your profits until the twenty thousand dollars you owe me is paid. Or, in case something should happen to you, your share of the factory comes to me."

"You figuring on killing me to get it all?" Steve said furiously.

"Of course not," Neff said disgustedly. "That's just a legal precaution. You'll find it in almost any agreement with this much money involved. Now sign it."

"If Pa finds out about this, he'll burn the factory before he'll let me have it."

"He'd do that if he knew I was getting a third of it," Neff said calmly. "In fact, if we don't get rid of Larabee, you won't get it, anyway. I'm taking a big chance on this debt. I'm betting you'll get the factory and I'll get my money from thirty percent of your profits. Now sign it."

Steve glared at the paper than at Neff. "I won't do it," he snapped.

"Then I'll have to tell the vigilantes that you killed Kelly O'Brien."

Steve's face blanched. "I didn't kill him, and you know it."

"Try telling that to the vigilantes. They'll find out you were there, and they won't ask any more questions."

"You'd swing, too," Steve said. "You were there. Remember?"

"You don't think I'd trap myself, do you? I've got a way figured out. But if you don't sign this paper, you'll sure dance on air."

Steve glared at Neff, breathing hard. Neff wondered if he would try for his gun. He could see that the thought was in his head. But Neff was prepared, and Steve must know it. His eyes finally dropped, and he reached for the pen that Neff had ready.

Neff folded the paper and put it back in his pocket. He had one more trump card to play, and he slapped it down before Steve had recovered from the first blow.

"While you were sleeping yesterday afternoon, I heard that Larabee has figured out somehow that you're the one trying to kill him. He made no bones about what he plans to do. It will be you or him, Steve, just as soon as he gets back this afternoon from Fort Wallace."

Steve, numb from the first shock, accepted this new threat without an argument. "I'll get him first," he said thickly. "I need a drink now."

"I'll buy," Neff said generously. "But don't get soused like you did yesterday. You can't kill Larabee that way."

Neff stayed close to Steve throughout the day. He bought him a few drinks, just enough to loosen his tongue. Steve talked recklessly, which fitted nicely into Neff's plan. He bragged to anyone who would listen that he was going to kill Dave Larabee just as soon as he got back from Fort Wallace.

Neff didn't know just when to expect Larabee back in Sheridan, but he took precautions to make sure that Steve didn't run into him. It meant giving up his game at the Golden Eagle, but he didn't mind. He was playing for much higher stakes now. Shortly after noon, he took Steve to the hotel and kept him there.

When it was dark, Neff suggested that it was time to strike at Larabee. Steve was drunker now but still able to navigate by himself. He was at the point where he was willing to follow any suggestion.

Neff led Steve out of the hotel and down the street past the saloons. Twice Steve wanted to stop for more to drink to make him feel better and improve his gun speed, but Neff didn't want anyone to see him with Steve now, so they hurried on.

Neff led Steve almost to O'Brien's Warehouse. There they left the street, and Neff explained that Larabee would be coming from the O'Brien house soon. They'd jump him when he came past the dark corner of the warehouse.

While Steve was peering around the corner of the warehouse at the lighted windows of Tully O'Brien's house, Neff stepped back and drew the knife out of the sheath under his arm.

Steve never knew what hit him. Neff planned it that way. He didn't want any noise. He used the knife twice more to be sure he had done a thorough job, then he wiped the blade and put it back in its sheath.

Quickly then, he turned and hurried up the street. In three minutes he was at his card table and had a game going.

It was almost an hour later that Pete Cottier came puffing into the saloon, his eyes wild as he looked over the tables until he located Neff. Coming over, he dropped a hard hand on Neff's shoulder.

"Steve's dead," he said. "Somebody knifed him."

Neff looked up, showing the surprise he had rehearsed. "Who did it? When did it happen?"

"Happened just tonight," Cottier said. "Down by O'Brien's Warehouse. Nobody knows for sure who did it, but they figure Larabee did. Steve's been spouting off all day that he was going to kill Larabee when he got home. Looks like Larabee beat him to it."

Neff pulled out of the game for a couple of hands.

Drawing Cottier off to one corner, he played his last trump card. "I'm not too surprised at what happened. I heard that Larabee had found out who two of the raiders were who hit his camp on the Smoky Hill. He swore he'd get them both. Even named Steve and you."

"Me?" Cottier croaked. "How could he know I was there?"

Neff shrugged. "How did he know that Steve was there? But he obviously did. Steve's dead, ain't he?"

"I'll kill him!" Cottier said after a moment. "I'll meet him in the street and gun him down if I have to."

"I'd try to catch him when he wasn't looking if I were you," Neff warned. "But if you don't kill him, you're going to stretch a rope, that's sure."

"The vigilantes will never hang me!" Cottier said vehemently, fear cracking his voice. "I'll kill Larabee first."

"Be sure you do," Neff said, "no matter how you have to do it."

Cottier nodded numbly and headed for the door, almost staggering. Neff watched him, thinking that this time he would surely succeed in killing Larabee because he was certain his own neck was the price he'd pay for failure.

Neff hoped that Cottier would do the job quickly. Right now the town was willing to believe that Larabee had killed Steve Gleye. Neff didn't want to give Larabee a chance to prove that he didn't. If Larabee never got to talk, then there wouldn't be any possibility that Neff would somehow be found out and accused of knifing Steve.

Once Larabee was dead, Neff would make sure the

vigilantes found out that Cottier had killed him. Cottier would swing for that, and Neff would be free. There'd be no one left alive who could connect him to all the deaths he had been involved in.

He'd have to make sure then that Tom Gleye didn't live long enough to change his will or even to find out that Steve was dead. This paper that Steve had signed would give him that Toledo factory. He was sure he wouldn't have gotten the factory as long as his two bungling partners were alive. To win this hand, he had to make sure both of them were dead. Half of that mission was accomplished now.

CHAPTER 14

Dave Larabee had spent most of the return trip from Fort Wallace planning his moves when he got to Sheridan. There were five soldiers with him this trip, one of them detailed to drive Julio Romeriz's wagon.

He had two pressing chores. He intended to find out who killed Romeriz, if possible. In a way he felt responsible for the Mexican's death because he was sure that knife had been intended for him.

He also had to locate the lawyer, Clyde Voss, if he was still in Sheridan. He didn't have any idea what the lawyer wanted to tell him, but the message had taken on added significance when he discovered how Slip Neff and Steve Gleye were maneuvering to keep Voss from seeing him. In the back of his mind the thought nagged at him that there could be some connection between the lawyer's disappearance and Romeriz's death.

As soon as the wagons and teams were taken care of at the soldier camp, Larabee headed for Tully's warehouse. If anything important had happened while he was gone, Tully would know. But Tully had little news.

"We buried Romeriz today," Tully said. "Nobody has any idea who killed him or why."

"I think somebody was trying to kill me and got Romeriz instead," Larabee said. "The same thing might have happened when Kelly was killed, too."

"I supposed they were just after the hides, then," Tully said.

"They didn't have to kill anybody to get the hides," Larabee said. "Have you heard anything about the lawyer who came in the day I left?"

Tully shook his head. "I haven't heard anything about any lawyer."

Misti came up the back steps of the warehouse. "You'll be here for supper, won't you?" she asked Larabee.

"Of course he'll stay for supper," Tully said.

Annie was just a step behind Misti. "If he goes somewhere else for supper, I'm going to make him take Misti with him."

Larabee looked at Annie. "Why?" he asked innocently.

"Because she won't eat if you're not here. You ought to see her when you're gone. She says she's worried. She—"

Annie was interrupted by Misti who had wheeled on her little sister. "You get back to the house and finish supper," Misti ordered.

Annie didn't question the thinly hidden threat behind the words, but turned and dashed down the steps. Tully grinned after her.

"She makes her conclusions pretty plain, doesn't she?" he said.

"Pa!" Misti exclaimed. Then she turned and ran down the steps, too.

Larabee understood Misti's embarrassment. But

instead of sympathizing with her, he was hoping that what Annie had said was true.

Larabee had planned to start his search for the lawyer immediately, but now he decided to postpone it until after supper. The search had waited for two days; another hour or two wouldn't make much difference. If the lawyer hadn't left town yet, it wasn't likely that he'd be leaving before the train went out tomorrow. The only other way he could get away would be to take the stage to Denver, and that wouldn't be leaving until tomorrow morning, either.

Larabee was shocked again at supper at one of Annie's astute observations. She had either been prying into his personal affairs or had overheard things not meant for her ears.

"That corporal had a girl at the party last night over at Bates's house," she said, looking out of the corner of her eyes at Larabee.

"What corporal?" he asked, although he already had an idea.

"Koonce," Annie said. "He had this girl who's staying at the hotel, Brenda Bailey."

Larabee shrugged. "Any reason why he shouldn't have?"

Annie's face lit up. Larabee realized she had been baiting him to see his reaction. Odd, now that he considered it, that he didn't really care. Obviously that was exactly what Annie was hoping for.

"Who is Brenda Bailey?" Tully asked.

"Somebody you shouldn't ask about," Mrs. O'Brien said.

"Oh," Tully grunted, looking from his wife to his daughters. "One of those things. Dave, let me tell you. If you ever get married, don't ever open your mouth when your women are talking about other women."

Larabee grinned and went on eating, hoping the subject was closed. But Annie wasn't through with it yet.

"Brenda Bailey is the girl who came here to get Dave," she informed her father. "But Misti has beat her out."

"Annie, shut up!" Misti said sharply. She got up and hurried to the stove to check on the pots there. All the supper, however, was already on the table.

"Young lady," Tully said sternly, "if you don't learn to control that tongue, somebody's going to cut it out someday."

Annie didn't seem overly alarmed. She grinned at Misti's back. "Misti might try it, too. But I was only telling the—"

"That will do, Annie!" Mrs. O'Brien said sternly. Annie subsided into silence.

Larabee finished his supper quickly. Misti hadn't gotten over her embarrassment, and, to save his life, Larabee couldn't think of anything to say that would relieve the situation.

Supper over, he put on his hat and headed up the street. If Clyde Voss was in town, he'd likely be in the hotel. But Larabee was sure that Steve and Neff wouldn't let him just walk in the front door and talk to him. They'd be watching.

Nearing the hotel, Larabee ducked into the alley behind the buildings and came to the hotel from the rear. He climbed the steps to the door that let him into the hallway on the second floor.

Larabee thought of going down to the desk and

looking at the register. But he was sure that Voss's name wouldn't be on the register even if he was here. The clerk might tell him something, but it wasn't likely. Neff and Steve had gone to great pains to keep Voss hidden; they wouldn't overlook a loophole like the clerk.

It was early enough that few people would be in their rooms yet. He checked down the hall, trying the doors. Most were open and the rooms empty. Two had people in them who resented the intrusion of a stranger. One door was locked solidly, something unusual for this hotel, Larabee thought.

The locked door intrigued him. There was no one in the hall, so he crouched by the door and listened. After a minute, he was rewarded by the fall of footsteps inside. He knocked lightly on the door.

The footsteps stopped, and there was a deathly silence for a minute; then the steps moved to the door.

"Who is it?" a timid voice said.

"Dave Larabee. I'm looking for a man named Voss."

"Larabee?" Excitement lifted the voice behind the door. "I'm Clyde Voss. Can you get me out of here?"

"Don't you have a key?" Larabee asked.

"Do you think I'd stay in here if I could get out?" Larabee thought for a moment. "I'll get a key."

He glanced at the number. Turning, he hurried along the hall and went down the steps. He looked for Steve or Neff but didn't see either one. At the desk, he asked the clerk for the key to Room 24. The clerk's eyes widened; then he shook his head.

"That room is rented. The renter has the key."

"You've got another one," Larabee said. "I want it."

"I can't do that," the clerk said.

"Then I'll break the door down," Larabee said, and started to turn away.

"Wait a minute," the clerk said in haste. "That's the only room in the hotel we can lock securely. I can't let you break that lock."

"You can save it by giving me the key," Larabee said.

He watched the clerk, wondering if he would reach for a gun. If he did, Larabee resolved he'd use his own. The time for reason or restraint was past.

The clerk, however, showed no inclination to fight. "They'll kill me if I give you the key," he said finally. "But if you take it when I'm not looking, there isn't much I can do about it."

Larabee nodded, running his eyes over the rack of keys hanging behind the clerk. Number 24 was there.

"Turn your head," Larabee said, and reached for the key.

Getting the key in his hand, he looked at the clerk who was searching on the floor as if he had lost something. Larabee turned and headed for the stairs.

When the key turned, the lock and the door swung open; the little man with the thick glasses was standing only inches away from it.

"Dave Larabee?" he said, holding out his hand.

Larabee gripped the lawyer's hand, surprised that it was a firm grip. Nothing about the little man looked solid.

"I had a telegram from my uncle saying you were coming and would have a message for me," Larabee said.

"Tom didn't want to write or wire what he had in mind," Voss said, moving back to the bed and sitting down. He looked nervously out the door. "You won't let them lock me in here again, will you?"

"I hadn't figured on it," Larabee said. He stayed in the doorway where he could see down the hall to the top of the stairs. "What did Uncle Tom have to say?"

"A confession, first of all," Voss said. "I have been his lawyer for a long time. You see, when your parents were killed by the Indians, they didn't leave you penniless as Tom made you believe. Your father had started a shoe factory in Toledo, and he didn't sell it when he started west. He had planned to have all his tools shipped to California and set up his factory there. Tom has handled the business since your father's death, taking all the profits from it."

"Do you mean I legally own a shoe factory in Toledo?" Larabee asked.

"Exactly. Tom built up the business and planned to leave it to Steve when he died. But Tom and his son had a terrible argument just before Steve left Kansas City. Tom had second thoughts and decided finally to do the right thing and turn the factory over to you. That's what he sent me out here to tell you."

"How did Uncle Tom get his hands on the factory in the first place?"

"Tom was the administrator of your father's estate. He took in the profits himself and never let you know you had a factory. He knows how much Steve is depending on inheriting that factory, which, incidentally, would sell for a small fortune now, and he was afraid Steve would intercept any letter he sent to you. He couldn't say everything in a telegram that he wanted to, so he sent me."

Larabee thought of all the things he could do with the money that factory would bring. Going to Toledo and running the business was something he didn't even consider. Suddenly another thought hit him.

"What would happen to that factory if I wasn't alive?"

"According to your father's will, it would go to Tom Gleye in case of your death," Voss said.

"And Tom is almost dead now. That means Steve would soon inherit it."

"That's right," Voss said. "What does that have to do with it?"

"A lot," Larabee said, seeing the picture at last. "I've come mighty close to being killed three or four times the last few days. I didn't know who to blame then, but I do now."

"Steve?"

"Who else? What would that business bring if I sold it?"

"Close to twenty-five thousand," Voss said without hesitation. "In fact, I have an offer of twenty-two thousand five hundred if you want to sell."

"I'll consider it," Larabee said, suddenly thinking of Brenda and her ambition to live in a city. But Brenda's ambition faded before the sparkling blue eyes of Misti. What would Misti like? He couldn't imagine Misti's making any demands about where or how she would live if she really loved a man.

"Can you find a place where I'll be safe from Steve and that gambler?" Voss asked.

Larabee thought for a moment. "I think Tully O'Brien will take you in till we can get you on the train back to Kansas City. Nobody will bother Tully."

"Good," Voss said. "Let's get out of here. Steve or

Neff might come back to check on me. They do that every little while."

Larabee nodded and went out into the hall with Voss. Carefully, Larabee locked the door. "Now you stay here till I return this key," he said. "We'll go out the back way. I don't want anyone to see us leaving the hotel."

"I understand," Voss said.

Larabee returned the key without a word, and the clerk said nothing. Then, climbing the stairs again, he led the lawyer out the back door and down the outside steps. Staying in the alley behind the buildings, Larabee picked his way through the darkness past the piles of cans and rubbish until he had passed the general store. Then he came out on the street and crossed the tracks, soon reaching O'Brien's house.

"Don't tell anybody about that factory in Toledo," Larabee warned Voss just before he knocked on Tully's door. "That's nobody else's business."

Voss nodded as Tully opened the door. Larabee explained who Voss was and his need for a safe place to stay.

"You say Steve Gleye is one of the men keeping him prisoner in the hotel?" Tully said when Larabee finished.

"Steve and the gambler, Slip Neff," Larabee said.

"He won't have to worry about Steve Gleye any more," Tully said. "He was found murdered just a few minutes ago. Right over by the corner of my warehouse."

Surprise jolted Larabee. "Murdered? Do they know who did it?"

Tully shook his head. "Some men say they heard

him bragging in the saloons today that he was going to kill you before you killed him."

Larabee frowned as he realized the implications of that. "I started looking for Voss as soon as I left here. I've been with him ever since I found him."

"Of course, everybody here knows you didn't do it," Tully said. "But I was just telling you the story that is spreading around. If you'd killed him, it wouldn't have been with a knife in the back. That's how he got it."

"Voss will be my only witness as to where I was," Larabee said.

"He can't say what you were doing before you went to the hotel," Tully said. "Neither can I. But I'll stand by you."

A knock sounded on the door, and alarm showed in the faces of the women. Annie ran for Tully's rifle, which he kept in the corner. "I won't let them come in," she declared stoutly.

"Put that away," her mother said sharply. "Pa will handle this."

"That gun would knock you through the far wall if you fired it," Larabee said, trying to break the tension.

Misti came to stand close to Larabee while Tully moved to the door and opened it. Zeke Quincey stood there, a shirt in his hand.

"Come on in, Zeke," Tully invited.

Quincey stepped inside, grinning at Larabee. "Figured I might catch you here. I found out who this belongs to." He held up the shirt.

"That's the shirt with the missing button, isn't it?" Larabee said, taking the garment.

"Sure is. I found it again in Steve Gleye's room. It's the same size as Steve's other shirts, so it must be his."

Larabee nodded. "I reckon it is, all right."

"He's the one who killed Kelly?" Tully asked sharply.

"He was on the raid," Larabee said. "I think the big man actually killed Kelly while the fellow wearing this shirt was wrestling with me." He held up the shirt to show the missing button, then fished the button out of his pocket.

"That proves that Steve Gleye was one of the murderers," Tully said. "Too bad he's already dead. But we'll find the other two now and hang them."

"Better keep quiet about this shirt," Larabee said. "If the people find out about this, they'll be surer than ever that I killed Steve. This would be a good motive."

Tully nodded. "You're right about that." He turned to Quincey. "Hear any more talk up town?"

Quincey nodded. "Plenty. Some people are getting pretty riled up. I figure somebody is talking too much. Probably that gambler who was with Steve a lot, Slip Neff."

"Likely," Larabee agreed. "Did you find any extra money in Steve's room when you were getting this shirt? Somebody should have the money that my hides and teams and wagons brought."

Quincey shook his head. "I didn't see any money. Of course I wasn't looking for money."

"Listen!" Annie said suddenly, and ran to the window and peered out. "A lot of men are coming. Pa, they may be after Dave."

"Could be," Tully said. "Dave, you get back in the bedroom where they can't see you when I open the door. I'll do the talking."

Misti caught Larabee's hand and tugged him into the bedroom; she stayed there with him while Tully opened the outside door.

Sound washed in from outside as the murmur of voices carried clearly into the bedroom. Above the rumble Larabee heard one voice speak out authoritatively.

"We figure he ought to stand trial, anyway. If he's innocent, we'll find it out."

"I happen to know where he was every minute," Tully lied. "I'll vouch for him. I'll guarantee you this much. He won't leave town till we clear up this matter. But let's find the right man before we hold a trial."

"I say we ought to try him right now," another voice said shrilly.

Larabee could almost feel the pulse of agreement throb through the crowd. Even Tully O'Brien might have trouble stemming that tide.

CHAPTER 15

"Where is he?" one man yelled.

"Where you won't get him till you cool off," Tully said sharply. "I promised you he won't leave town, and he won't. If you're so set on trying somebody for murder, find the man who killed Kelly."

There was more murmuring, but apparently Tully O'Brien's opposition to a trial for Larabee carried a lot of weight. Larabee was surer than ever now that Tully was the actual leader of the vigilantes. He was a good man to have on his side, that was certain.

While Tully continued to talk to the men outside the door, Larabee got to wondering about Steve's murder.

"What reason could anyone have had for killing Steve?" he said, surprising Misti who was listening intently to what was going on out by the front door.

"Evidently people think you're the only one who had a reason," Misti said. "Since Steve bragged he was going to kill you, they think it makes sense that he tried and you killed him. I'm scared, Dave."

"Steve must have come down here looking for me, all right," Larabee said. "Still, I wouldn't have believed he had that much nerve unless he was drunk."

"Could he have thought you had a reason to kill him?" Misti asked.

"He would have if he'd thought I had identified him as one of the men on that raid on the Smoky Hill."

Outside, the noise of the crowd began to subside, and soon it was quiet. Tully turned to the bedroom door.

"They're gone. Come on out."

"How long before they'll be back?" Larabee asked, coming out with Misti.

"I think they'll sleep on it," Tully said. "Once they do that, they'll use their heads tomorrow and know that you're no murderer."

"Not everybody sees things as clearly as you do, Tully," Mrs. O'Brien said. "Especially when they're riled up like they are."

Tully sighed. "I reckon somebody is stirring them up, all right. If we can find out who is doing that, we might have the killer. He may want the vigilantes to hang Dave before anybody figures out he's innocent. The real killer would sure go free then."

"Dave isn't going to sleep in the warehouse tonight," Misti said flatly. "They might sneak back and look for him there."

"Misti's right about that," Tully said.

"He can have my bed," Annie said. "I'll sleep on the floor."

"Like fun you will," Larabee said. "I'll stay in the house if you want me to. But I'll bunk on the floor."

Quincey went back to his cot in a tent hotel, and Clyde Voss bedded down on the living-room floor. Tully and Larabee sat up an hour past bedtime to make sure their visitors didn't return. Then Larabee rolled up in some blankets Misti had gotten for him and went to sleep.

He was awake before dawn and was up fully dressed when Tully came in to start the breakfast fire.

"What do you plan to do this morning?" Tully asked.

"I'm going to look for Neff," Larabee said. "Neff and Steve seemed to be working together. If Steve got the money for my hides and wagons, it's a good bet that Neff has that money now. He has a way of getting his fingers on any money that is around."

"Do you think that Neff was on that raid that killed Kelly?"

"I don't know," Larabee said. "I never thought that Neff would venture away from his card table for anything. But he was with Steve and those two buffalo hunters when the Indians ran them into our supply wagons headed for Fort Wallace. If he'd go on that trip, he just might go on a raid like the one on the Smoky Hill."

"Maybe we ought to put him on trial. When he has to be a witness, he might admit something."

"I doubt it," Larabee said, shaking his head. "Neff's a pretty slick character. He wouldn't say anything to trap himself even if he was guilty."

"I suppose not," Tully said with a sigh. "I want to find the man who killed my son so bad I guess I don't think straight."

"If we can find that big buffalo hunter, I figure we'll have the man you want," Larabee said. "He came from the other wagon while I was fighting with Steve, so he's the one who must have killed Kelly."

"We'll find him," Tully said. "If we were sure that Neff was along on that raid, we'd jerk him up, and we'd make him tell who the hunter was even if we had to burn his toes off."

Larabee was probing every possibility like a chess player while he ate his breakfast. The family was quiet; even Annie had little to say. It was as if everybody were waiting for something to happen.

With breakfast over, Larabee checked his gun carefully, then put on his hat. Misti was at the door when he reached it.

"Be careful, Dave," she said. "You know somebody in town is trying to kill you. I think it would be better if you let Pa look around for the man you want."

Larabee shook his head. "I know Neff, and I know the questions I want to ask him. This is my job, not your pa's."

"Don't pass any alleys without looking into them," Tully warned. "There are plenty of men in town who ain't above shooting or throwing a knife from a dark corner."

"You don't have a very high opinion of your town," Larabee said.

"I know it better than you do," Tully said. "Why do you think the vigilantes were started? The only law this town knows is the fear of the rope. Take that away and nobody would be safe."

"I'll watch my back," Larabee said, and went outside.

He glanced behind him once and saw Misti still standing in the doorway watching him. Maybe Annie was right about Misti's feelings for him. It gave him a warm glow just thinking about it. He'd never had that feeling about Brenda. There had been nothing mysterious about Brenda's desires. If she wanted something, she let the world know about it. She had wanted Larabee and had played her cards to get him. But when she couldn't bend him to her will, her disenchantment had been just as obvious as her desire had been before.

Larabee moved out on the street. It was early, and the street was still quiet. It struck Larabee that it would be his chore to let Tom Gleye know that Steve was dead. Maybe Neff had already sent him a telegram, but Larabee doubted it. It wasn't likely that Tom Gleye knew that Steve had any dealings with Neff other than to gamble with him.

He thought of Neff and realized he wouldn't be an easy man to corner. Neff would just deny he knew anything about any hides, and Larabee couldn't prove otherwise. The gambler hadn't accumulated his wealth by being easy to handle.

Larabee moved past the Otero & Sellar Warehouse across the street from the general store. A man was sweeping off the front platform at the warehouse, but he didn't even look up as Larabee passed. The Golden Eagle Saloon was just across the tracks from the section house, but there was no stir at either place. The train had been turned around and was down by the water tank now getting ready to make its return run to Kansas City.

Larabee watched the Golden Eagle as he passed. That was where Slip Neff spent most of his time gambling. It was too early for him to be there now unless he was waiting for Larabee. Larabee wasn't sure just why he felt that Neff would be laying for him somewhere, but the feeling persisted.

On Larabee's right was the Bull Head Saloon. It was closed, too, but here was one of the places where the element who would kill for hire hung out. Larabee couldn't be sure that somebody hadn't been hired to kill him.

Passing the Bull Head, he moved on toward the hotel, staying on the south side of the track. Neff should still be there, and if Larabee could catch him just as he got up, he might get something out of him. It was worth a try. Anything was better than waiting for something to happen.

As he passed one of the big tents that were used as cheap rooming houses, he saw two men come out into the morning light. The cots were only a quarter a night, but the men had to look elsewhere for breakfast. These two were obviously doing that right now.

Larabee looked at them just as he had been looking closely at every man he saw on the street this morning. One of the men was the big buffalo hunter, Pete Cottier, who had been with Steve and Neff when the Indians had chased them over to the freight wagons between here and Fort Wallace.

The big man stopped and stared at Larabee for a moment, then turned and dived back inside the tent. Larabee, alerted by the sudden move, hurried on but kept one eye on that tent flap.

A few seconds later, the man appeared again, a gun in his hand. Larabee was some distance from the tent now, but even at this distance he could see fear and hate mingled in the man's big face.

The man jerked up his gun and fired, the sound a violation of the morning's stillness. The suddenness of the move and the distance between the big man and Larabee apparently saved Larabee. The bullet snapped harmlessly past his ear.

A dozen things flashed through Larabee's mind in the next second. His hand dived for his gun, but he realized that he didn't dare shoot at Cottier, for he was standing now right in front of the tent. Very likely there were fifteen or twenty men inside.

He was next to the railroad grade with a street between him and any building. He felt like a sitting duck. The grade was about three feet high here where it went through town. If Larabee was on the other side of that, he could get out of sight of Cottier.

He scrambled up the steep side of the grade as another bullet thudded into a tie within inches of his side. Then he threw himself over the rails and slid down the other side. Wheeling around, he lifted his gun and peered over the rails.

There was no one in front of the tent now. After missing with his first two shots, Cottier apparently felt he had to have more protection.

Larabee lifted his head a little higher to get a better view of the area on the other side of the tracks. Heads were poking out of doors and tent flaps, but Cottier was not in sight.

Then suddenly a bullet struck a rail just to one side of Larabee and ricocheted past his head and over the buildings and tents behind him.

Larabee ducked involuntarily. But he had spotted the place where the shot had come from. Apparently Cottier hadn't considered the tent any protection at all and had dived around behind the little frame real-estate building next to the tent. This building had done a great business at first, but as the tracks moved southwest toward Fort Wallace, the sale of lots in Sheridan had come to a halt.

Poking his head up again, Larabee shoved his gun above the rails and fired at the corner of the real-estate office. An answering shot thudded harmlessly into the grade as Larabee ducked below the level of the rails.

Larabee snapped another shot at the building, then slid down to the bottom of the grade. Getting to his feet, he crouched as low as he could and ran to his left several yards. Behind him, he heard another bullet plop into the dirt just below the level of the rails.

Panting from his run, Larabee dropped on the slope of the grade again and inched his way to the top. Peering over the rails, he saw Cottier at the corner of the building peeking around at the spot where Larabee had been. Even from this angle, he was only partially exposed to Larabee.

Cottier was shifting around uneasily. Obviously he was beginning to wonder why Larabee wasn't returning his fire. Larabee had to act quickly to take advantage of his move.

The distance to the real-estate office was greater now than it had been from the spot where Larabee had first dived over the tracks. He knew he'd be lucky to hit any part of the exposed portion of the big hunter's body.

Aiming as carefully as he could, he squeezed the trigger. Cottier was slammed backward from the corner where he rolled out into the open. Larabee was ready to fire again when he saw that Cottier had lost his gun in the fall. He wasn't dead, but without a gun, he was out of the fight.

Leaping up, Larabee scrambled over the railroad tracks and ran toward the little building, holding his gun ready in case Cottier came up with another weapon. But Cottier only glared at Larabee and made no move to get to his gun. Larabee doubted if he knew where it had fallen.

When Larabee reached Cottier, the big man was holding his hand tightly over a hole in his side from which blood was oozing between his fingers. A half-dozen men came running from the sleeping tent when they realized the shooting was over. Two of them lifted Cottier gently and carried him into the tent, while a third one went in search of Dr. Epstein.

Larabee followed Cottier to the tent and was about to go in when Tully O'Brien came puffing up.

"Who was that?" Tully demanded. "Why was he shooting at you?"

"I intend to find out," Larabee said, pushing past the tent flap.

Tully was just a step behind Larabee. "Did you kill him?"

"Just put a hole in him," Larabee said. "He'll live."

Larabee went on to the cot where they had laid Cottier, Tully close behind.

"Why did you try to kill me?" Larabee asked Cottier bluntly. "I never did anything to you."

"You were fixing to," Cottier said. "Get me a doc, will you?"

"They've gone for Dr. Epstein," somebody said.

The doctor came in then, his shirt only half-buttoned. Larabee guessed he'd been sleeping late. He looked over Cottier, then opened his bag.

"Who shot you?" he asked.

"He did," Cottier said, indicating Larabee.

"He jumped me for no reason that I can figure," Larabee said when the doctor looked at him. "I'd sure like to know why."

"Won't talk, eh?" the doctor said, and started to work on the hunter, ripping the shirt away from the wound. He took a bottle from his bag and gave Cottier a long drink from it. He repeated this twice during the time he took cleaning and bandaging the wound.

"That should do it," he said when he had finished. He looked at Larabee. "I think he'll tell you what you want to know before long."

Larabee grinned as he realized what the doctor had done. He'd given Cottier enough whiskey to loosen the tongue of a stone statue.

Larabee watched Cottier a while, then Tully stood watch while Larabee went outside. Tully came out after a while.

"He's talking," Tully said. "But the whiskey is working fast. He'll be out cold before long. Doc must have given him more than he can handle." He looked down the street. "There's somebody at my warehouse. I'll have to go. But I'll be right back."

Larabee went inside and moved up to Cottier's cot. "Who told you I was after you?" he asked.

Cottier looked at Larabee with glassy eyes, his mouth twisting around into the mockery of a grin. "Who do you think? Slip said you were on to us."

"About what?" Larabee asked.

Cottier shook his head. "Oh, no, you don't. You ain't tricking me into telling everything. Slip says you already know it was him and me and Steve that waylaid you on the Smoky Hill."

Larabee hid his surprise. "Sure, I know that," he said. "Did Neff think you'd go free if you killed me?"

"Sure," Cottier said, and Larabee realized the big hunter wasn't going to make sense much longer. "You know something else," he said, his words running together. "He knifed Steve down where you live and figured you'd be blamed for it. I was going to kill you before you had a chance to prove you didn't do it." He laughed, more of a gurgle than a laugh. "Now ain't that something?"

"It sure is," Larabee agreed.

Cottier rambled on, something about shooting at buffalo bulls and Indians. Larabee knew he wasn't going to get any more information out of him now. But he didn't really need any more. He had to find Neff before Neff learned what Cottier had said.

Cottier was the man who had killed Kelly. But it had been Neff who had masterminded the whole thing. It was Neff who wanted Larabee dead. Somehow he was maneuvering things to get that shoe factory in Toledo, Larabee guessed. Taking Neff would be like trying to catch an angry rattler with his bare hands.

CHAPTER 16

Larabee left Cottier's cot and hurried to the front of the tent. As he stepped outside, he almost bumped into Tully coming in.

"Did he say anything?" Tully asked.

Larabee nodded. "Plenty. He admitted being on that raid so he's the one who killed Kelly."

Tully reached for the flap of the tent, but Larabee caught his arm. "You can't go in there and murder him. You'd be dragged up before the vigilantes yourself."

Tully breathed hard for a moment, then nodded. "You're right. The vigilantes will handle him. Who else was on that raid?"

"Steve and Slip Neff. Neff is the brains behind the whole thing. He killed Steve, hoping I'd get blamed for it. Then he sent Cottier to kill me before I could prove I didn't kill Steve. That way nobody would ever investigate Steve's murder any further."

"Clever sidewinder," Tully grunted. "Now let me give you some advice. Don't you try to kill Neff. Just catch him and the vigilantes will do the rest."

"I won't kill him unless he tries to fight. But I figure he will."

Larabee swung up the street again to the hotel. He went to the register and flipped it around to see the

number of Neff's room. Number 25, the register said.
The clerk objected, but Larabee ignored him and
took the steps three at a time.

As he had half expected, Number 25 was empty.
The door was ajar, and Larabee pushed cautiously
inside. Somebody had left in a great hurry. Some of
the bedding was on the floor, and the drawers had
been jerked out of the bureau. Larabee found a tie
and a shoe that had been missed.

Larabee guessed that Neff had been awakened by
the shooting. Since it had taken place across the track
from the hotel, Neff would have had a good view of
what went on from his window. Apparently he had
seen Cottier go down and had decided that his safest
course lay in getting out of town fast.

Larabee went back into the hall and down the
stairs as fast as he had come up. There were only two
ways that Neff could get out of town, by train or
stagecoach, unless he rode a horse. And Larabee
didn't think Neff was much of a horseman.

As he came out into the street, the train was pulling up from the water tank to the depot directly
across from the hotel. It gave a warning whistle to
call the passengers aboard. There were only four cars
and a caboose. Two cars were loaded with hides, and
the other two were passenger coaches.

Larabee moved down behind the train where he
could watch both sides. Neff was already out of the
hotel, but Larabee was betting he'd show up in time
to get on the train.

Several passengers came out of the hotel and got on
the train, but Larabee didn't see Neff. When the
train gave a final whistle before starting the drivers,
Larabee became alarmed. Had he missed Neff some

way? He was still positive the gambler would try to go out on the train. But only seven passengers had gotten aboard, six men and one woman. All six men were bigger than Neff.

Running forward, Larabee reached the front passenger coach and swung up on the steps. The passengers had all gone into this car. The conductor stopped Larabee at the door.

"Got a ticket?" he asked.

"I'm not going anywhere," Larabee said, pushing roughly past the conductor.

"Then get off," the conductor shouted, turning to follow Larabee into the car.

Larabee looked over the seven passengers. Apparently the other car was empty. It might be filled up before the train got to Kansas City. Or it could be that it took two cars to bring people out here to Sheridan but only one to carry those who wanted to go back.

Larabee scanned the passengers. The woman was in the back of the car, and suddenly she got up and began moving toward the rear door that would let her out on the car's platform.

Something about her movement caught Larabee's attention. Like the kick of a mule, it hit him. That was Slip Neff. Small as he was, Neff could easily pass for a woman in size. If he had remained seated, Larabee doubted if he would ever have given him a second look. But now he knew him, and he yelled for him to stop. Neff dived through the door and down the steps.

Larabee started running down the aisle, but the commotion caused the men to turn to see what was going on, and one of them threw his feet into the aisle. Larabee tripped over those feet and banged his head on one of the seats.

By the time Larabee had recovered his balance, Neff had disappeared into the hotel. The train started moving and Larabee had to hurry to get down the steps. The train was gaining speed as he jumped to the grade and slid down to the level of the street.

He ran inside the hotel, but the lobby was empty. Expecting that Neff would go back to his room to get rid of his woman's disguise, Larabee went up the steps in long bounds, barely glancing at the clerk's startled gaze.

Neff's room was empty, but there was a woman's hat and veil on the floor and a long shawl close by. Larabee didn't see the long skirt that Neff had been wearing, but he was sure the gambler had discarded that somewhere by now.

Turning, he ran to the back stairs. Throwing open the door, he looked down the alley. There was no one there, but he caught a glimpse of someone disappearing around the far corner of the Cross-Tie Saloon. Larabee went down the steps three at a time and ran to the corner of the saloon. Caution slowed him just before he went around. Neff would know he was being followed and might lay for him somewhere. Neff wasn't likely to make many more mistakes.

Peeking cautiously around the corner he saw that the alley along the side of the saloon was empty. He ran to the front of the building in time to see a horse being spurred up the street. It was a full three seconds before he realized that the rider was Neff. He hadn't supposed the little gambler could ride a horse like that.

A man charged off the saloon porch where he had

been peeking in the window. "Hey, that sidewinder stole my horse!" he yelled. He fired a shot after Neff, but Larabee knew he had missed. Larabee hadn't even taken his own gun out of its holster.

There wasn't another horse at the hitch rack. In fact, the saloon wasn't even open yet. Larabee turned to look for a horse. Down in front of the general store there were two horses racked. He began running that way.

Neff was almost to the end of the street before Larabee reached the store. The shot that the angry owner of the horse had fired had brought people into the street to see what was going on.

Larabee saw Neff reining up down by O'Brien's Warehouse just as he reached the store. He didn't see what had stopped Neff, but he tried to take advantage of the delay. He grabbed the reins of a horse and started to mount.

"Hold on," a man on the store porch yelled. "You can't have that horse."

"I'll bring him right back," Larabee promised. "I've got to catch that man."

"Not on my horse," the man shouted and lunged at Larabee.

Larabee couldn't waste time now trying to explain the situation. He wheeled and met the man's charge, slamming a fist into his chin. The man staggered back, and Larabee followed up with another blow that stretched him out on the porch. He hesitated only long enough to make sure that the man was not armed, then leaped into the saddle and wheeled the horse into the street.

Neff was past the warehouse now, galloping toward the river. But he had someone in the saddle with him. Larabee could see that it was a girl. That would be Annie. He supposed Annie had dashed out into the street at the sound of the shot and had stayed there when normal caution would have sent most people to cover. Neff had apparently taken the girl as a hostage.

As Larabee came even with the warehouse, Misti came charging around from the barn on her pony, riding bareback.

"That man kidnaped Annie," Misti shouted. "We've got to get her back."

"I want him, anyway," Larabee said. "But be careful. He's sure to have a gun, and he's not afraid to use it."

"Who is he?" Misti shouted as she matched the pace of Larabee's horse.

"The man who killed Steve Gleye," Larabee shouted back.

Ahead, Neff splashed across the creek. Annie's yells came back to Larabee and Misti. Larabee would have found it amusing if it hadn't been so serious. Annie wasn't scared; she was mad. That could mean trouble for Neff if he only knew it.

Neff didn't take the regular trail to the south that went around the twin buttes as Larabee expected him to. He started straight on along the side of the railroad track. There was a deep cut ahead where the graders had slashed through a sharp ridge to give the roadbed a steady rise. Here Neff had to swing his horse to the southwest, which took him up along the edge of the dark rock covering the northeast slope of the twin buttes.

"Go right down the tracks," Larabee shouted at Misti. "If he tries to swing back, you can beat him there. I'll cut him off to the south."

He was sure that Neff would swing to the south now. The going was too rough to the west for a horse carrying double. He wanted to get Misti far enough away that she'd be safe when Neff turned to fight. He would fight. Larabee was certain.

Splashing across the ford, Larabee turned his horse to the south to cut Neff off if he turned back from the slope of the buttes to the main road. Misti pounded straight ahead. She'd have to slow down to get through the cut, but she could make it faster than she could go around the way Neff had started to do.

Larabee soon saw that he had guessed right. Neff had realized his mistake in attempting to follow the railroad tracks and was now trying to get back to the main road to Fort Wallace. Larabee urged his horse to a faster gallop as he closed in on Neff. Neff had lost too much time, and the double burden was slowing his horse.

Neff apparently saw that he was going to be cut off, for he reined his horse back up the slope, forcing Larabee to leave the road and take to the slope himself.

Larabee gained on the gambler steadily, and finally Neff stopped his puffing horse and wheeled around, his gun in his hand. Larabee yanked back on the reins and threw himself from the saddle. The gun in Neff's hand roared just as a scream echoed over the hillside.

Larabee jerked his gun clear and looked over the saddle of his panting horse. He wouldn't dare shoot while Annie was with Neff. But he saw that Neff had his hands full. It had been the gambler who had screamed. Annie had sunk her teeth into Neff's wrist while he was aiming his gun, and she was still wrestling with him.

Larabee started running up the slope as he saw Misti coming up from the north. As soon as Misti had seen where Neff was going, she had turned toward him. Up on the slope, Neff had lost his balance in the saddle as he fought Annie, and now he was struggling to keep from falling off the horse. The horse was too tired to pay any attention to the struggle taking place on his back.

Neff lost his balance finally and fell off his horse, landing on the rocks with Annie on top of him. Larabee was climbing as rapidly as he could. When Neff got free of Annie, he'd almost certainly come up shooting. Larabee hoped that Annie got away from him quickly. Larabee was out in the open now, and couldn't shoot back.

But Annie had no intention of getting away. She was still biting and kicking, and Neff had all he could do to protect himself. When he finally struggled free of the girl, Larabee was within ten yards of him. Neff took one look at Larabee, gun cocked, and threw down his own gun.

"Good work, Annie," Larabee praised.

Annie was still furious. She aimed one more kick at Neff's shins. "I'll teach you to carry a girl around like a sack of flour!"

Misti rode up then and dismounted, running to Annie and throwing her arms around her. Larabee moved over and picked up Neff's gun. Then he searched the gambler and took a knife from a sheath under his arm.

"We'll walk back," he said. "Get started."

Without a word Neff began moving down the slope. Misti and Annie brought the horses. At the river Larabee guided Neff up on the tracks to cross the water, while Misti and Annie rode the horses across the ford. There were several men, including Tully O'Brien, waiting on the other side of the river.

"Let's lock him up and ship him out on the train tomorrow," one man suggested.

Tully didn't say anything. Both the train and the stage had left for today. Before another day came, the vigilantes would have time to meet.

"Before you lock him up, I want the money he got for the hides and teams and wagons he stole from me," Larabee said.

"There was a bundle of money in his suitcase," one man said. "The conductor threw it off when the train pulled out without him. Some of that may be yours."

"I can tell you how much the hides brought," Tully said. "The livery man can quote the price of the teams and wagons."

"Where can we lock him up?" one man asked.

"I've got a spot in one corner of my warehouse," Tully said. "Sort of want to keep an eye on him, anyway. Need his testimony to convict Cottier."

Once Neff was securely tied up in the warehouse, the crowd dispersed, and Larabee had a chance to talk to Tully.

"I suppose the vigilantes will meet tonight," he said.

"You can lay odds on that," Tully said with satisfaction. "We've got two murderers to try. The rope still rules Sheridan, and it will show its authority tonight."

"Cottier is shot up," Larabee said.

"Not too bad to hang," Tully said, and Larabee knew that neither Cottier nor Neff would see tomorrow's sunrise.

A man brought in Neff's suitcase. Tully counted

out the amount of money that he had paid for the two loads of hides while Misti and Annie came in to watch.

"You can start buying what you planned to buy now," Tully said.

"First I'm going to buy a dress for Annie."

"For me?" Annie squealed. "Why?"

"Kelly had planned to buy you a dress," Larabee said. "I can't take the place of your brother, but I can buy you a dress."

"You'd make a wonderful brother," Annie said. "That's what you're going to be, too, ain't it?"

"Annie!" Misti exploded.

Tully laughed. "Annie, I think we'd better go count the ties in the railroad track."

Annie went reluctantly, and Larabee grinned at Misti. "Let's go to the store and buy Annie a dress."

As they went up the street, Larabee told Misti about the shoe factory Clyde Voss said he owned. "Now I've got a question," he concluded. "Do you want to be the wife of a shoe manufacturer or the wife of a freighter?"

"Do I get a choice of the man?" Misti asked.

Larabee shook his head.

"In that case," she said, "I'll settle for being the wife of Dave Larabee. I'll let him be whatever he wants to be."

They were right in front of Otero & Sellar's Warehouse in full view of the whole town, but he stopped and kissed her long and passionately. He didn't care what the town thought. In fact, he didn't care what anybody thought as long as Misti was happy. And the look in her eyes told him that she was.